Unveiling Love

A London Regency Suspense Tale:
Episode II

Vanessa Riley

Books by Vanessa Riley

Madeline's Protector

Swept Away, A Regency Fairy Tale

The Bargain, A Port Elizabeth Tale, Episodes I-IV

Unveiling Love, Episodes I-IV

Unmasked Heart, A Regency Challenge of the Soul Series

Sign up at VanessaRiley.com for contests, early releases, and more.

Published by BM Books

A Division of Gallium Books

Suite 236B, Atlanta, GA 30308

ISBN-13: 978-1-943885-10-7

SAVING A MARRIAGE OR WINNING THE TRIAL OF THE CENTURY

Dear Lovely Reader,

Unveiling Love is a serialized historical romance or soap opera told in episodes. Each episode averages three to eight chapters, about 18,000 to 30,000 words. Each episode resolves one issue. Emotional cliffhangers may be offered, but the plot, the action of the episode, will be complete in resolving this issue.

My promise to you is that the action will be compelling, the romance passionate, and the journey like nothing you've read before. I will tell you in the forward the length. This episode, Episode II, is eleven chapters long, 40,000 words. Enjoy this Regency Romance.

Vanessa Riley

Winning in the courts, vanquishing England's foes on the battlefield, Barrington Norton has used these winner-take-all rules to script his life, but is London's most distinguished mulatto barrister prepared to win the ultimate fight, restoring his wife's love?

Amora Norton is running out of time. The shadows in her mind, which threaten her sanity and alienate Barrington's love, have returned. How many others will die if she can't piece together her shattered memories? Can she trust that Barrington's new found care is about saving their marriage rather than winning the trial of the century?

In this episode:

Barrington Norton has always despised lies and has formed his life upon a foundation of truth. Yet, discovering the truth of Amora's past sends him to the breaking point. How can he ever make amends for not believing her? Will she ever love him as she once did?

Amora Norton is tired, tired of fighting for her marriage and her sanity. Now that she understands how fleeting Barrington's love is, she wants none of it. It may be better off being alone than living with pity. Having lost all, can she find herself?

Nonetheless, a serial abductor is at large, awakening to existence of the one that got away. Only a united couple can put an end to his reign of terror.

Sign up for my newsletter at www.vanessariley.com or www.christianregency.com. Notices of releases, contests, my Regency Lover's pack, and other goodies will be made available to you.

Dedication

I dedicate this book to my copy editor supreme, my mother, Louise, my loving hubby, Frank, and my daughter, Ellen. Their patience and support have meant the world to me.

I also dedicate this labor of love to critique partners extraordinaire: June, Mildred, Lori, Connie, Gail.

Love to my mentor, Laurie Alice, for answering all my endless questions.

Love to Sharon & Kathy, they made me feel the emotion. You're never second place in my heart.

And I am grateful for my team of encouragers: Sandra, Michela, Felicia, Piper, and Rhonda.

CAST OF PRIMARY CHARACTERS

Barrington Norton: a barrister by trade, he is a free-borne mulatto gentleman of a wealthy black merchant's daughter and a landowner's ne'er-do-well son.

Amora Norton: the wife of Barrington Norton. She is of mixed blood, the daughter of an Egyptian woman and a wealthy Spanish apple merchant.

Smith: a man convicted of coining.

Cynthia Miller: a songstress and sister of Gerald Miller.

Gerald Miller: Barrington's best friend who saved his life during the Peninsula War.

Mr. Beakes: Barrington's solicitor.

Vicar Wilson: a minister serving at St. George

* * *

Duke and Duchess of Cheshire: the newly married William St. Landon and Gaia Telfair

Mrs. Gretling: an abigail to Amora.

James: a man-of-all-work to Barrington.

Mr. Charleton: a rival of Barrington from their youth.

Chapter One: The Road to Answers

Rain splashed against the glass of the carriage as it rumbled down the road. Amora sat on her hands across from Barrington. Barely a word exchanged between them since their harrowing flight from London at dawn.

He'd caught her asleep on the floor, but his anger at the fight at his patroness's home must've made him forget. Good. He'll have a lot more to understand once they arrived at Tomàs Manor.

In another hour or so, Mother would give him answers he'd never expect. Sleeping on the floor wouldn't seem so bad, but would Barrington understand? Could a man ever fully understand being made a victim, knowing other victims? Could he ever accept being so low and helpless? Never. Not Barrington.

She glanced at him again. His bruised countenance bobbled as his head zigzagged and zagged along the seatback. His snow-white cravat fluttered with each short snore.

He hadn't shaved. Not how he liked to start his day with light stubble edging his chin. At least he'd changed his clothes from his soiled evening pantaloons and coat.

Oh, that dreadful party. His reputation must be in tatters. What would be the repercussions for a mulatto, a black, striking a member of the ton?

A sigh left her like a billow used to stoke flames, only she had none. Her fire was gone. He didn't believe her, just like mother. The man she loved thought her wanton.

And how could she forgive him constantly being with Cynthia? How strong of a man could he be with a tart constantly trying to give him pie? Even a self-righteous man could get hungry.

She pushed at her brow, trying to remember what happiness was. It wasn't in the carriage, or London. Certainly not with Mother. Yet, did happiness exist with Barrington, being with him, being married to him? She could count the days on one pinky, the moments she didn't fret over his opinions, his wants, his desires.

With her middles stewing, she balled her fists, hiding the unnumbered fingers. When he discovered how wrong he was to believe Cynthia's lies, could Amora ever fully trust that he'd never have another moment in which doubts about her honor would win?

With a shake of her head, she turned to the window and the endless streams of water. Surely, that must be a bad omen. Yes, his god was still angry with her. Maybe mother's Isis was too.

"Gerald, no!" Barrington bolted up. His grey eyes were vacant, then beset with heavy blinks. He rubbed his face and peered out the window. "We are getting close. Pity to visit Mrs. Tomàs on such a wet day."

"Weeks away from yuletide, she'll probably be too busy with things. She'll not care. Besides, she's used to me showing up looking like a drowned rat. If she tries to get us to stay, don't agree."

His lips thinned as he tugged at his lapel. "Rat? What does that mean and explain last night, too? Why did you come to the ball? And why were you alone with Charleton?"

"That's a lot of questions. A famed Barrington Norton interrogation." She folded her arms about her cape. "Why don't you explain yourself? Why did you not want me to go, and why were you embracing Cynthia Miller? No, I forgot. The accused can't ask questions."

He leaned back as his frown lifted in a smirk. "Clever. Madam judge can ask questions of a barrister. I have nothing to hide. I do apologize for causing a scene. I simply lost my head when I saw you with a rake."

"No other explanations?" She tilted her head forward. Her heavy heart made her wobble a bit. "You touched a peer, an innocent one. The ramifications--"

"I'll deal with that. My short absence might be warranted, but I doubt Charleton will do anything of it, for it will expose him too and you. He's so fond of you."

She held her irritation at his lack of belief in her inside. "Well, Cynthia Miller will miss you. And don't deny it. I saw you two."

"What?" He rubbed his jaw. "So that's how Charleton tricked you, with jealousy? She's very emotional right now. Caught in some trouble, but my investigator will solve that."

Amora tried hard not to roll her eyes to avoid seeing the growing pile of stupidity and hopelessness building in her skull. "Always helping others. That jade won't bother Beakes. She finds reasons to be around you. Can't you see she's in love with you? That she'll use anything to twist you up, to compromise you?"

"Preposterous. She's Gerald Miller's little sister. I need to protect her. Miller saved my life. I owe it to him."

Barrington leaned forward. His smirk increased. "So out of jealousy, you went alone with a rake to the garden. Convenient of him being able to give you a tour."

"I thought..." She turned her head and tried to search for the right words to convince him, but the old spire of the priory came into view. A chill raced through her down to the boning of her corset. She had intended to paint it before her abduction. That horrible day - grabbed out of her slippers, beating on masculine arms that had to have been forged in iron - stuck in her head. One. Two. Hard to breathe.

Something caught her hand.

She jerked away, only to witness Barrington's concerned pout. He'd joined her on her seat. "We could go straight to Cornwall. A couple of notes at the next post off to Hessing, and we could start anew."

He put an arm about her back, toyed with a raven curl poking from her bonnet. "You just have to pay the price." Pulling closer to her ear, his whispered breaths kissed her lobe. "Just the truth, Amora."

How dare he?

How could he try to seduce her into a lie, because he couldn't accept the truth? She stiffened, tried to push away, but he crowded her. How ironic. She usually crowded him.

"Please, Amora."

His sweet strong voice made her want to curl up in his lap and retreat into the safety of his arms like last night. But, could she pay the price? She didn't have any more lies to give, just ugly truths.

With a shake of her head, she said no and shoved on

his chest. "Go back to your seat, Barr."

His grey eyes smoldered. He lifted her palm and put his lips to them. "Don't you want to start anew? Pay the piper. Own your lies, all of them."

Pulse rising, pounding in despair, she wrenched away. Hurt at his words and her terrible weakness for him. "Stop it. I'm not in the mood to be bedded and then dismissed again."

Barrington blinked and sat back. "Amora, I am ready to hear your side. I'll forgive anything. I just need the truth."

"Go to your seat. Take your suspicions with you."

Hands in the air, he lunged to his side of the carriage. "I'm trying to make this easier for you. There's vanity in falsehoods. It's best to own our mistakes."

"My own flesh and blood, the woman who birthed me didn't believe me. Why should the man I wed?"

She looked to her lap and folded her hands beneath the creamy wool of her stole. Only a stranger, Vicar Wilson, and perhaps, Mr. Charleton understood. She slumped against the window and counted tufts of white silk lining the carriage walls. "Mother will tell you what you want to know."

Until this moment, she didn't realize how similar her Mama and Barrington were. No wonder neither loved her enough.

Gunshots rang out.

Barrington's gaze shot to the carriage window. The rain had stopped but low clouds still filled the sky. Traveling on the back roads held a certain amount of danger, but he always rode prepared.

He ran a finger along the knob fastening the

compartment under the seat. James kept a gun oiled inside and stocked with plenty of bullet packets. He'd protect his wife from bandits. No one would ever have a chance to hurt her again. No rake or bandit.

Another gun belched. The sound was a high pitch squeal. That was a small weapon, one not built for war or highwaymen. He eased back onto his seat.

Amora rubbed her temples. "Mother must be practicing her pistols. She hasn't done that since Papa... in a long time."

As the carriage came to a stop, he spied Mrs. Tomàs traipsing from the orchards toward the large house. Her raven hair bounced with each step. The simple straw bonnet did a poor job of keeping her tresses orderly.

Coming from the direction of the big stable house, the unusual woman, with skin almost as dark as his, carried a flintlock and dangled it by her side. So unlike the fastidious lady of his memories, the one who belittled his stature, his race, his personal small fortune absent his grandfather's wealth, even his father's waywardness on their last meeting. For Amora, Henutsen Tomàs had wanted a man of noble blood like the Charletons or truthfully any white gentleman of means.

The heat in his lungs started to burn his nostrils. He extended his arm to Amora. "Last chance."

Chin high, she pushed past him and plodded up the steps to the wide portico. "Let's be done with this."

His feet became weighty lead. He held onto the door of the carriage. His plan to learn the truth no longer seemed like a good one. How much worse would he feel when Mrs. Tomàs confirmed his suspicions?

Or even worse.

What if she didn't and Amora had truly been

abducted, how would he make up for his lack of trust?

Thunder clapped. He tensed adding pressure to the bullet wound in his hip. A just reward for acting like a jealous fool and riding hours in a carriage. Shaking out his leg, he eased to the ground. "James, refresh the horses in the stables. This could take awhile."

His man nodded and moved the carriage forward. Barrington hurried and caught up to his wife.

"Mr. Norton, Amora? What are you doing here?" His mother-in-law set her gun down and wiped her hands on the sides of her dark colored walking dress. "I would have prepared something had I known."

Barrington step forward and bowed his head. "We've come to ask you questions."

"He came to ask questions." Amora moved behind him almost as if she hid.

What could she be afraid of? Mrs. Tomàs wasn't much taller than she. They shared similar body weights, nothing to fear.

"Mr. Norton, looks like you caught the bad end of a fight. But you look well, dear." The older woman swiped at her face and held her arms open, beckoning with a nod for Amora to come.

Her daughter bristled and stepped away. She slunk to the corner and clung to one of the whitewashed posts supporting the covered roof. "Tell Barrington what happened."

Her voice sounded short, hot like fire. Then it died away in the increasing wind. She played with the buttons on her cream redingote. Three people stood on the portico. How could it be possible for her to feel so alone?

Mrs. Tomàs retrieved her shawl from a chair sitting against the wall. "I've missed you, sweetheart. Let me get the cook to make you something to eat."

Undoing the strings of her egret feather bonnet, Amora kept her focus toward the thick grove of trees, the start of the Tomàs Orchards. "Get the papers. Show him."

Tears dribbled down his mother-in-law's stoic face as she moved near her daughter and stroked her back. "Are you sure?"

"Yes. Barrington, follow her." The tone smoldered again, short, punctuated, determined. "Ask your questions. Find your truth."

He adjusted his spectacles. Part of him wanted to embrace his wife and tell her he'd changed his mind, but that wouldn't stop his questions. No, only the truth would.

He took note of her stiff posture, her expressionless gaze toward the trees. She didn't seem like one fearing exposure, but she didn't cry out her innocence either.

The Old Bailey would convict her.

Hadn't he?

Releasing a deep breath, Barrington trailed the gun-toting pharaoh Tomàs into the house, but stopped at the door. "This will be over in a few minutes. Then we'll start again."

Amora's gaze never strayed from the orchard.

His pulse slowed. No longer sure of anything, he hesitated to enter the house, but powered inside. They would begin again no matter what.

The aroma of baking crust filled the entryway. Apples must be baking in a pie. Proud Mr. Tomàs, God rest his soul, he loved this land and proclaimed his pippin fruit trees made the best desserts. Barrington's mouth watered, but not enough to wet the desert called his soul.

The old pharaoh would soon confirm Amora's lies. She'd strayed with Charleton. They were too cozy last night in the garden. He'd punch the man again for tempting her.

Mrs. Tomàs peaked out a window facing the portico. "She looks well. It's been so long since I've seen her, not since the wedding breakfast here. Five years is a long time."

Barrington tapped his boot. He and this woman weren't friends, but if Amora wanted her she could've sent for her. "Show me the papers. Then tell me why you allowed her to marry me without disclosure. That could be thought of as a breach of an implied contract."

Dark eyes, smaller than Amora's stared back at him. Her lip trembled, but then she flicked her stubborn chin up. "If you are here to give her back, I'll take her. I'll care for her, much better than you ever could."

For better or worse, Amora was his. Even if she lied, even if she still refused to admit the truth. "The papers, madam."

"Wait here. They are in Mr. Tomàs's study."

She disappeared down a hall.

Barrington swiveled his head from side to side, taking in the drawing room. There were three garniture vases on the mantle, which Mrs. Tomàs called oinochoes. Dark mystical vessels, maybe taken from the foot of the pyramids, probably where she stored her excess hate.

Barrington paced across the square tapestry filling the floor, just as he'd done as he'd waited for Mr. Tomàs to grant Amora's hand in marriage. He claimed to like Barrington, but he surely made him stew, sitting as silent as stone, puffing on his pipe, listening and weighing the reasons he should allow his youngest daughter to become engaged to a soldier bound for war.

Barrington rubbed his hand on the back of Tomàs's Chippendale chair that still sat close to the fireplace. For a moment, the air filled with the scent of missing tobacco. He stared at the hall waiting for Tomàs's big hat with the foot-wide brim to materialize. The house lay too quiet without the big man's laughter. It must've been a terrible time for Amora and her mother when the big-hearted Tomàs passed.

Putting a hand to his hurting eye, Barrington shook his head. This place steeped in sadness wasn't for his wife. It felt unhealed, almost deathly. Maybe the grieving never vanished from these walls.

Dropping onto the large brownish divan, he released a clogged breath. Every muscle hurt. His head throbbed. Riding in a cold carriage for hours made the aches worse, all because he allowed his jealousy to devour his logic, devour his discipline. No more.

He'd take Amora away to Cornwall, immediately. There, they had nothing but pleasant memories, walks along the white cliffs, waltzes in the sweet sea air. There she'd be able to tell him the worst, even admit her unfaithfulness with Charleton. Barrington would forgive her, and she'd forgive him for dragging her here.

She'd been faithful to him for five years. Nothing else mattered. They'd recommit and begin anew. If he hurried they could get pretty far before the storm gave its worse.

Prying from the too comfortable chair, he walked to the door, purposing to scoop Amora up, apologize, and do so all the way to Cornwall.

"Mr. Norton? You're not leaving." The pharaoh's voice sliced through him, making him feel stupid. "You came for these?"

With his hand latched onto the knob, he took a breath and turned the brass. Freedom and forgiveness, his and Amora's future stood on the portico.

"You can't leave yet. Amora asked me to give these to you. I have to do what she wants. I can't fail her again. You must look at these papers. You'll know everything. All the facts."

Mrs. Tomàs's tone tugged at his scales of justice, resetting and swaying his innards, everything that made him what he was, a man who fought for truth.

"These will tell you what happened. You come unannounced and now you want to go away without seeing them?"

Of course, he craved ripping through the thick folds of paper resting within her fingers, but was there more barrister in him than husband, more law than love? He leaned against the door, his head poised to ram the painted wood.

Mrs. Tomàs came to his side and shoved the pages against his palm. His index finger automatically curled onto a corner.

"There you go, Mr. Norton. These are the physicians' accounts of Amora's condition when she escaped and…" She took a big gulp of air as if something wrapped about her throat strangling her, "and their harsh treatment of my poor girl."

Escaped? Treatment? Seizing the paper, he turned and moved deeper into the room, stopping under a brass sconce. The light made the ugly words plain. He shuffled through record after record and almost punched the wall as he'd done Charleton's lip. "They pushed her off a table? Tied her to a bed." He couldn't read any more. His shaking hands couldn't hang on to the paper. They dropped, dusting the floor like ugly snowflakes. "Why would they do this? Why did you allow such cruelties? Why?"

Mrs. Tomàs, the stone pharaoh, cried loud, throaty, noisy sobs. "I didn't know they'd do that. My husband's cousin, he said he'd handle things. He said it was a safe place out of the public eye for her to have the baby."

Baby?

Amora had Charleton's child.

Barrington clutched at his chest as if that would hold his heart inside, but nothing would. He wiped his mouth against his sleeve. "What happened to the infant? Did you foist Amora's only living baby onto some relation to stave off shame? I'd have taken her and the by-blow, you miserable shrew."

"There was no baby." The pharaoh crumbled into Mr. Tomàs's throne. "No baby at all. Amora babbled when she crawled onto the portico. So swollen from the salted pig scraps her abductor fed her, we all thought she was with child. So he…we sent her away to protect her reputation."

All Amora's difficulties in carrying a child to term, could it arise from this barbarism? "What type of woman are you? Is there no Christian decency in this family?"

"Is it Christian for you church goers to look down on the ones who made a mistake? Is it Christian to label the babes, by-blows?"

He put a hand to his floundering cravat wishing to wring his neck for such poor words. It wasn't right what he'd said. It was a common slur to slap folks into a box. He of all people should know better.

Mrs. Tomàs took a lacy handkerchief from her pocket. "You know the stigma of having a baby out of wedlock.

My husband was gone. His cousin said she'd go through the laying-in there, and then he'd bring her and the child back, but Amora wasn't pregnant. We let those English witch doctors hurt her. They tortured my girl all over again."

Barrington's thoughts and stomach churned as he analyzed this new evidence. An abused Amora with a shaky testimony led to her being sent away at the cousin's urgings. Perhaps Charleton wasn't the villain. He hid his aching fist, the one eager to punch again, behind his tailcoat. "Where is this cousin? Perhaps he abducted Amora and used your grief and naivety to cover his crimes."

"He's dead. Died this time last year. Amora refused to come back to Clanville for his burial."

Barrington's mind flashed to a moment, twelve months prior. He'd caught Amora crying, shivering in her chambers with a note scrunched up in her hand. She said it was nothing. She'd said nothing of a funeral or this.

He rubbed his brow trying to remember dates. Hadn't her nightmares become more frequent last November? The headaches surely started. He thumbed his temple. "Don't defend a beast to protect the Tomàs name. He should've been made to pay."

"It wasn't him. He was in Spain, then the Indies when Amora disappeared. I had him picked up from the docks a week or two before she escaped and made it back to this house. Couldn't have been him."

The pharaoh's head shook so hard it might fall off. "No, it wasn't him. And I don't blame him anymore for what I let happen to Amora. But I swear, Mr. Norton, if I had known, I would never have allowed her to be put in that asylum. If I'd been stronger, I could've been a better help to her."

His hatred of his mother-in-law melted a little at the agony in her sobs, the rushes of water pouring from her eyes. He folded his arms trying to hold together his shattered logic.

"I did wrong, Mr. Norton. I should've believed her and found another way to help." She dabbed at her face again. Maybe even a crocodile could shed real tears.

Yet, if it wasn't the uncle who had taken Amora, who was the fiend? Too much training at the Lincoln Inn swirled in his gut, and Barrington swiveled to his first conclusion. The beginnings of his wife's disappearance had to be a seduction and according to the law, any consent would set the villain free, the poor woman blamed. "You were always pushing the Charleton brood on Amora. Admit it was one of the dowager's sons."

"It is true. I wanted Amora with one of them. Not being English in England is hard. You need a fortified stomach."

He ran a hand over his brow, adjusting his lenses. "What on earth are you speaking of, woman?"

"You care too much to please them, you know?"

"And you don't?"

"When I came from Carthage with Mr. Tomàs, I saw how things go here. I did everything to keep a spotless reputation, but nothing more. I don't eat at their trough, but they seek mine out. No one has apples like the Tomàs's. I know my worth. You don't. That's why you are in here now, and not with Amora."

The woman knew how to shove a knife in the soft spot betwixt his ribs, inflicting the most damage. Leaking fury with each breath, he whipped up his court voice, loud and strong, the one that boomed over the juryman's ruckus. "While this treatment is abysmal, it doesn't prove Amora was abducted, only what happened after she returned and how horrible of a mother you are."

He bent and picked up a few pages and rolled them within his fist. "Tell me what you know. With whom had she become smitten? Tell me of her lover. I won't be angry with Amora not with all she's been through. I can even understand her not telling, not wanting to relive a minute of this. I just need the truth. Was it Mr. Charleton or his brother, the earl?"

"Mr. Norton, you're not listening. My sweet *habibi*, my poor heart didn't run away. I tried to get her to like the Earl of Clanville, but he became reclusive after his carriage accident. His brother, the jovial Mr. Charleton never captured Amora's attention, not even for a minute. She never betrayed you."

Thunder cackled as Mrs. Tomàs came closer. Her eyes wide. "My youngest daughter didn't run off. Someone took her and locked her away for weeks in a very dark place."

"Darkness? Amora's fear of the dark, her need to burn a thousand candles? This is from being imprisoned by an abductor?"

"Yes, just like the other girls."

Others? Blood rushed to his ears. Light-headed, he backed against the wall. His legs shook. Every organ inside his body slapped and twisted as truth broke free. "Others?"

Mrs. Tomàs tugged her shawl tighter across her limbs. "They'd found a milk maid dead a day or so before Amora returned. The girl had been tampered with. I mourned, sent my condolences, but didn't think more of the sadness. Then I heard the whispers about another girl, Clara Milton. Her story was the same as Amora, taken, kept in chains in a dark place. That's when I knew Amora had been taken."

A dead girl. Another witness. Similar stories. His brainbox slipped into a drunken dizziness as his thoughts spun. Every unnecessary disagreement about thrift and spent wax, three hour or eight hour candles, were all a cry for help. One Barrington never seemed to hear. "Why? Why didn't you tell me? When I came to redeem her? When we said our vows, you could've warned me."

"I wanted it all to go away. Amora was home and seemed in control of herself. It should be forgotten."

"But the rumors of her with Charleton?"

Mrs. Tomàs clasped her hands and dipped her head, hiding her wet black eyes. "I did nothing to explain her absence to Clanville. I didn't need too. They still bought Tomàs apples. You didn't believe her either. Isn't it easier to accept a lie than the horrible truth?"

The aches in his head, in his soul, raged. Amora wasn't seduced. He'd let Cynthia's gossip and his own jealousy ignore his wife's protests.

He adjusted his spectacles as if the motion would make the truth clearer, easier to accept. Amora was abducted, no euphemism. Cold hard fact.

And he'd swallowed a lie.

"The only good thing about sending Amora away was that they kept her restrained from suicide. The other girl took her life, not more than a month later. My heart weeps at Amora's pain, living through such horrors and not being believed by those close to her. Betrayed by her own mother."

His own heart dropped past his knees straight to the

floor. The organ, a mere pebble now, lay atop his boot, ready to be kicked and trampled to a deserving death. "I didn't believe her. If only she'd told me straight away. I'd--"

"I told her not too, Mr. Norton. That kind of thing didn't happen to a Tomàs. I should've gotten out of my sick bed and saw to her care. I should've held her through her nightmares. That's what a good mother would have done. Like you said, I'm not a good mother. With her older sister eloping and never returning to visit, you can see how well I've done."

She bent and started picking up the rest of the fallen pages. "The thought of you… It was the only thing she'd brighten for. Now you too have made her feel low."

The sound of Mrs. Tomàs's broken speech, her tortured confession drum, drum, drummed into his thick skull. It was as if Justice Burns pounded his gavel. Amora had truly been abducted. Others had been abducted as well.

How cruel Barrington must've seemed to Amora. This was worse than not holding her hand and comforting her when she miscarried.

And it wasn't God's fault.

Only Barrington's.

Making his obstinate hip obey, he rushed to the threshold and turned the knob as he should've done minutes ago. Amora must forgive him. She had too.

He thrust the door open. Out on the portico, his nostrils filled with the clean scent of rain. *Oh, God. Give me the right words to say.*

He whipped his head to the left, then to the right toward the stables.

Vacant.

Amora had disappeared.

Chapter Two: Fleeing the Pain

Another roar of thunder sounded. The small sun escaped from behind a cloud and shone brightly as water poured from the heavens. Amora scanned the rare sight, a celestial war in the clouds. Something to behold from Papa's oak.

The tree stood a few miles off on the far side of the orchards.

When was the last time she'd climbed it? Maybe ten or twelve years ago. From its boughs, she'd first spied Barrington. He was rescuing his friend Gerald Miller from the wrath of some older boys. She knew then he'd grow up to defend his friends.

Just not his wife.

She wanted to cry, but she'd done that enough. Wasn't there enough rain trickling down her cheeks to suffice?

Needing to be as close to Papa as possible, Amora trudged deeper into his orchards. Being amongst the Pippins, she almost made out Papa's laugh blending with the thunder, almost felt him leading her forward. Memories of apple picking with him, of singing about his oak covered her broken heart. "Papa, you loved me. Do you love me still?"

The wind picked up chilling her face, tickling her chin. She breathed the fresh, sweet air in and out. Away from the house, Barrington's hoarse complaint of *doesn't prove Amora was abducted* could no longer be heard. What did he need, to find her dead at the monster's hands?

She ripped off her gloves and let the water hit her palms. The rain didn't feel cold anymore. Swirling a pinkie and then an index finger around her palm, she painted the lines. If only her hand exposed a map, something to indicate where to go.

The path couldn't lead to Mother or Barrington, anywhere her word wouldn't be believed. She knew that now.

With arms outstretched, she savored the richness of the fresh air, the wet pines. The green fingers of bittercress plants waved, shedding light petals, kisses in the breeze. Pink-tinged flowers of anemones flopped upon her slippers. Water leaked onto her stockings. She plucked a leaf, rubbed it between her finger and thumb. It oozed sticky jade pigment but the paint washed away with the rain.

The shower meant nothing. It wouldn't impede her love of this place. She was home on Tomàs land. Papa was so proud of the rich earth. Wouldn't his oak look glorious today, whipping its boughs in this storm?

She yanked off her bonnet and let the rain kiss her countenance. Sprinting, far and fast, deeper into the orchard, she followed this true love, dancing upon the sloppy leaves squishing beneath her feet. Nature, the only god whose love was constant, called her home.

A mile or two in the mud quickly passed, faster than

counting the days hoping to feel secure within her marriage, or awaiting Mrs. Gretling's confirmation that enough months had passed to know Amora was increasing with Barrington's babe. Barrenness should be preferred to loss.

Her low heart moaned. Her cold teeth chattered to the rhythm of the pianoforte playing in her mind.

The weight of her bland redingote now sodden with water slowed her steps and trapped her arms. Nothing would trap her again. Not the expectations of her mother or the demands of being Barrington's perfect wife. Nothing mattered anymore. She shook free, leaving the coat to the mud.

Thunder's percussion accompanied Haydn's Symphony, the last duet she played with Papa the night before he died. Oh, Papa. *I'll always miss you. If only you were here.*

Her wet chignon began to unravel. The silver pins popped out, sending soggy tresses down her back. Amora didn't care. She took a few steps, then a few more up the ravine where the oak stood.

"Papa!" She parted her lips, and yelled again at the top of her lungs. She drank the sky's nectar.

The deluge quickened. Her nostrils filled. She could no longer breathe. The landscape obscured in front of her. "Is this another trick? Providence, will you steal my way to the oak? Maybe you'll have me fall off the ravine."

Clouds bumped and blotted out the light. A shudder of confirmation raced her spine. Maybe Providence wanted her to die. Maybe it was time for that. For what did she have to live?

Barrington's love was all she had. She'd even traded in

her self-respect to be perfect for him, but Amora should've known this day would come. Hadn't there been proof of it with his love for paperwork and Cynthia?

She blinked her wet eyes and tried to make out the surest path to Papa's oak. Past the orchards, the thick woods shrouded cliffs and rocky ravines and sometimes a swirling river. Papa bought the land cheap for nobody thought he could make a go of it, but mother's know how and stubbornness made the difference. She said if she could grow pomegranates, she could grow apples. She showed everyone.

And Papa so loved her. He fought against prejudice and her pride to love her. Why couldn't Barr be the same, completely accept Amora?

She trudged a little farther and slipped. Her shoe went flying but no thud answered. The ravine.

One of Barrington's tortured verses trickled into her remembrance, Though He slay me, I will yet trust Him. "Why? Why trust someone who will slay you?"

"And why not slay me now?"

No more pain or sorrow.

No more being a burden.

No more wrestling with second place to anyone or anything.

The fretting ended today, and she wouldn't be a coward about it either.

Fire in her lungs, she stood up tall, lifted her chin and moved forward. Her stockings became more wet, her toes colder in the loose mud. When her foot felt nothing in front of her but a drop-off, she stopped.

Pushing back a lock of hair from her vision, she eyed the deep ravine. This part was surely high enough to break limbs, maybe snap a neck on a boulder below. If that didn't do it, the water below could finish her. Would the river be cold this time of year? Would it numb her to all the emptiness?

Didn't the doctor say jumping was preferable to slitting a wrist?

With her dead, Mother could lift her head high in the village and wear fancy mourning shrouds again.

And Barrington…he'd be free.

Even in the deluge, the thought of him with another made Amora's throat dry. Yet, the man didn't know what he'd married. So if he found happiness with Cynthia Miller, would that be wrong?

She stuck her foot out, but something inside, quiet and proud, made it drop back to the solid earth.

Thunder barked. She backed up from the ravine. Her cellmate, her lost friend Sa…Sarah. Hadn't they fought to keep hope alive even in the darkness of the cell?

Jumping wasn't keeping hope.

Sarah would be so disappointed in her.

Moving farther away, Amora stumbled and fell against a tree trunk, massive and wide. It was Papa's oak.

She turned and stretched her arm about the circumference. Springy bark tickled her chin. Overhead branches shielded her a little from the heavy rain. A sense of calm swept over her as if Papa offered a hug.

She ran her wet hands along the crevices of the bark. From the boughs of this tree, she'd count to five then jump into Papa's arms. He'd chide her for climbing and trespassing so close to the cliffs, then give her a big spin. Even as he got older, he could still catch her for she loved leaping out of the tree.

She put a foot on a gnarled root and lifted an arm to the high branch. If she got a hold of it, she could probably still scoot up the tree. Then she could pretend once more that her world was safe. Maybe she'd jump and reach the sky.

But no one was here to catch her.

No one.

Sobs strangled as she sank against the trunk.

The wind made the boughs of the tree wave. Her dripping muslin gown stuck to her skin chilling her. She rubbed her arms.

Like brush strokes, beautiful streaks of lightning sailed across the sky. The world moaned, and the clouds swallowed the brightness. It grew dark again. If only she could vanish like a flash of light.

She stood, lifted her face to the steady rain and walked to the edge of the ravine. The ground shifted. Some soggy earth dropped into the river. This time she'd ignore Papa's warning. And Sarah's too.

The rain beat an outline about her feet. Mud slunk around her, before sliding off the ravine.

She edged closer to the sky. Maybe Providence would take the ground from her, too. She'd have no complaints of the thief. Then it wouldn't be as if she'd jumped, just God finally finishing her, like he should have done back in that pit.

"Amora!"

Hoof beats sounded behind her. She kept her eyes on the flashes of light and refused to turn.

"Don't move, sweetheart!" Barrington motioned the horse through the brush. His gaze fixed on his wife.

James had tried to talk him into taking the carriage, but nothing could cross the orchards like a good mount.

With each shock of lightning, Barrington patted the

horse to calm her whinnying. If he'd been kinder to Amora, none of them would have to risk all in a storm. Why couldn't he stop the questions? No answer would change the past. He realized that now.

His leg swung out of the stirrup. He lost his balance, but clung to the reins, using everything within in him to reclaim his seat. It had been two years since he'd ridden. Now Amora's life depended on his skill.

Righted in the saddle, he braced and jumped a gully, but he'd fall off the beast a thousand times to save her. "I'm coming for you!"

Her tresses whipped in the wind. She did not flinch with the fresh crashes of thunder. The fear of being struck by lightning must've evaded her thoughts. With her body up so high, she could be a magnet for the storm's strike. *Dear God don't let her fall.*

So many emotions swelled within his gut, but none more than a sense of stupidity and helplessness.

He chose to have doubts.

He prosecuted the case in his head.

He let Cynthia's witness overshadow everything.

His jealousy of Charleton tainted Amora's protest.

He was guilty, so guilty.

Moving as fast as he could, he approached the precipice upon which she stood.

Hair hung down her back with twigs and leaves sticking to the delicate curls. The wet fabric of her dress clung to her shapely hips, her wondrous frame. She could have been Helen of Troy, the face that launched a thousand ships. That beauty too was abducted, but her husband fought to return her.

Not even a week ago, he'd caressed Amora and told her all was forgiven. Why did he let the gossip, his own insecurities challenge his resolve? "Don't move, sweetheart."

She didn't acknowledge him and kept looking off in the distance.

He looped the rein around a branch. Sucking in a breath, he eased off the gelding and hoped his hip would obey. Surprisingly, it felt looser. Hanging onto a horse might've stretched out the muscles, shifted the bit of bullet caught near the bone. He moved easier. His stride lengthened. A small blessing from the God he'd turned away from.

Trying not to startle Amora, he eased within three paces of her. The soggy ground beneath him sucked at his boots.

"Don't come any closer. I don't want you here." Her voice rose above the moans of thunder.

He stopped. She was too near the cliff's edge. "Come away with me."

She shook her head. With no coat or bonnet, rain drenched her solemn form. Her skin looked cold, ashen. She must be freezing.

He reached out a hand, and she took a half-step. The end of her one slipper dangled over the edge. Rocks broke away and dropped to the river below.

With haste, he lowered his arm. He couldn't make her more unsteady. "Turn to me. I'm sorry."

"For what? Marrying me. For getting you punched. Losing our child?"

The list of her charges was high. The breath in his lungs ignited, charring his chest. He forced a swallow to extinguish his bonfire of wrongs. "None of those things are your fault."

"Yes, they are. If I had told you what happened, you

could've begged off, made me release you from our engagement." She swiped at her chin. "You could work hundreds of hours or marry someone like Cynthia who could bear your heirs."

"I only want you. I believe you now. Fully. Completely."

"You are lying. I heard you say the papers weren't enough."

He hit his hat, shoving it tighter onto his skull. Such rotten words for her to have overheard. "You didn't stay for the rest of your mother's testimony. Mrs. Tomàs attests you didn't go willingly with anyone. That you never fancied Charleton or any other." As slowly as he could, he took another step toward her.

"Stay back." She inched further away. More ground dropped. She hopped, landing safely, but again near the edge. "I hear you coming. Just like the monster. I remember his dragging steps."

She could fall and die upon the rocks below or be pulled under by the currents and drown. Barrington's heart beat so hard and fast, but he needed his agile mind, too. "What did it sound like, Amora? Tell me. I'm listening."

She put her hands to her neck, rubbing the sides. "I'm not a good witness. Go back to London and stay with your truthful mistress."

"Move away from the edge, and I won't come closer."

Her head shook then stilled, returning to her stoic pose. "No more telling me what to do. My say is all that counts."

How could he convince her? All he had was the truth. It didn't seem enough. "I want no one but you. It's always been that way."

"Maybe before the war, not now. You suffered. My friend Sarah suffered. Sarah? What was her whole name? I should have given up then. Sarah would be safe from the monster." Amora gripped her temples, wobbled, then became stone again.

Another victim? And somehow Amora felt she could've saved her. There was no reasoning with evil or stupid barristers like himself. He advanced another foot. A few more inches, and he could grab her. Hopefully, they both wouldn't topple over. "Tell me how you could've saved her?"

"If I did what the monster wanted. He craved consent. Consent to be used."

Her words made everything inside cringe. The monster knew the law. He shook his head, swiped at his brow. "I can make this better for you. I'm desperate to save you. Let me."

"Will you kiss me and make it all better?" She tugged her arms about her chest and lowered her head. "Liar."

"Amora, I've never lied to you."

"Yes. Every time you said you were happy with me. You're lying now."

His fingers itched. Was he close enough to pull her to him? If he could, he'd caress her until he could prove how sorry he was. "I love you, Amora. And beg, beg your forgiveness. Please, babe. Babe, please."

She pulled at the sleeves of her dress, clawing at the wilted cap of the muslin. She let out a laugh that was so near a sob, it ripped his heart. "Of course you love me, so much so you run from my bed straight to Cynthia."

"It wasn't like that."

She ripped at her collar as if it burned. "I hate this color. I hate these bland colors. I wear them for you, thinking that would make you love me. Would you be my champion if I painted my face, smelled like rotting flowers, or actually have an affair?"

Amora was talking nonsense, but she was still talking. "I'll buy anything you want. Even green. It doesn't matter if I can see it or not."

"Why did I beg to stay true for you? I should've surrendered and stopped him from hurting Sarah. She would've been spared."

She lifted a foot. Her slipper dangled over the edge, before she stamped the ground. Mud flew staining her skirts. A clod fell off the cliff.

"I know you've been faithful. So have I."

"Where's the proof, Barrington? Your chrysanthemum laced cravats say otherwise."

Her evidence did seem worthy to convict, but he'd never thought of Cynthia that way. "I needed some time to puzzle things out. And I got it all wrong. But, I've never lied to you. If you had succumbed to the abductor, I would have understood. Blast it. I wish you had runaway with Charleton, if that could've prevented your abduction. I love you. As long as we love each other, anything can be solved. Oh, please come away with me."

Conflicted between tackling her and hoping for the best and trying to logic out something coherent enough to make her turn, he tugged at the buttons of his coat. "Wear my jacket. I don't want you chilled."

"Nothing matters. You'll change your mind tomorrow once Cynthia whispers in your ear."

"That won't happen. I know the truth now. You know I don't lie."

"Hence the rub. You won't move past my omission. I lied to marry you. I thought your love would take away the nightmares." Her head shook as she smoothed water from her face. "It won't. Pretend I'm lost. Go now."

He plodded another step, definitely within reach of her. A heavy sigh fled his nostrils, but he wouldn't be satisfied until she fit in his arms. "You don't need forgiveness. I need you to forgive me. You listened to your mother, and you didn't tell me. But, you know me. I needed the facts."

"How can I give them? A moment ago, I remembered Sarah's name. I have bits and pieces and most make no sense." She rubbed her temples. Raven tresses stuck to her cheek. "I have no more proof, no more strength."

Her shoulders sagged. "I'm tired, tired of hurting you and me."

Desperate, he latched onto her hand. "If you jump, I'll go too. I won't let you go ever again."

She hit at him, swinging wildly, until she knocked his spectacles from his face.

He didn't care. Barrington only wanted her safe. He pulled her soaked form into his arms. "Stop, Amora. We can survive this together. Maybe I can help you remember. We can figure out who did this to you and Sarah and make him pay for this crime. Then the nightmares will go away."

She stilled and leaned back as if to view his face. Her violet eyes opened wide. "Together, we could bring him to justice?"

"Yes, I'll make everything better." He kissed her forehead. "Please say we can."

"I don't know, Barrington."

"I'll fetch my glasses, and we will go from here. Together, we'll face this."

She didn't say a word, but she'd stopped trying to

wriggle away.

Good. She would accept his help. Feeling more confident, he loosened his grip along her waist to fetch his glasses.

Lightning crashed. The earth groaned.

Rocks snapped and shifted below her feet.

She pushed on his hip, shoving him to the ground as the cliff gave way.

Chapter Three: The Fall and The Fight

Just like jumping from her oak, Amora felt the air rush toward her. Her skirt billowed up her legs. Out of instinct, her arms lifted, and she clasped a tree branch, thick like Papa's arm. The river swirled below. The foaming tops lapped at the wall of dark earth forming the ravine.

"Oh, God, no!" Barrington's voice rumbled overhead. "Hang on, Amora."

When the ground crumbled beneath her feet, she'd pushed Barr with all her might so he wouldn't fall too. She had to save him.

Peering up, she saw his head crane overhead. She watched him stick out an arm, but he'd need another two feet of length to reach her.

"The horse's reins, Amora. I can use that to get to you."

"Don't. I can't hold on much longer."

"Try Amora. You can't die." His head disappeared.

The neighing of the horse sounded closer.

At least he sounded as if he believed her. That would

be a good last memory.

Shoulders aching, she closed her eyes, pointed her toes and let go.

Her skirts ballooned again as she eased into the swirling water. Dunked beneath the blues and greens of the waves, she kicked a little and brought her head to the surface.

The water moved fast from the swelling rain. It swirled her around and around like her first reel with Barrington. The rhythm shifted. The up and down, the bobbling of her body now met the beat of a pianoforte. Blinking, she could see Papa's hands holding hers against the keys. She lifted a palm to touch his fingers and swatted air, sprays of foam.

The river was warmer than normal. It soothed like the low heat of a bath that had gone tepid. A tingle coursed her spine, her toes. Her muscles relaxed. She allowed the water to carry her. Nature was her friend, the god she should worship. Maybe this god knew where she belonged.

A wave spun her. She could see the top of her oak, just the boughs and the thick emerald leaves. No sign of Barrington. It was best if he gave up.

Yawning, she lowered her neck and slipped below the water. Nothing but snow white and bubbling foam surrounded her. She lifted her countenance to the indigo sky. Her limbs whirled in the crest. The river swallowed her again, washing her face in the bluest water she'd ever seen. Shots of sapphire, hints of garnet and jade colored the bottom. Nothing had been so beautiful, not since Cornwall.

Her legs became heavy. Her arms stiffened. The minutes of being above the water dwarfed being dragged below. The pressure on her chest hurt. The pain in her temples throbbed. A voice grew louder, calling out her name.

Like music, the tones held a lilt. Then a flash of light exposed blond hair. Sarah's face, pale and small, mouthed *don't forget me*.

Another promise broken. They'd made a pact to stay together. It held until Sarah, fearing for her father's health, gave in to the monster's promises.

Her screams. How could Amora forget the girl's screams?

Shaking her head, Amora lifted her chin above the foam and gasped for air. There was still fire in this Tomàs girl. She had a promise to keep. Kicking as much as she could, she fought to stay upright.

The water sped up. Ahead, the river made a tight curve. Maybe if she worked against the current it would spit her out. She braced and pushed. Closing her eyes, she waited and almost prayed for another chance.

Her body lifted. Arms and legs flipped and twisted. The bend came and the river vomited her to the banks. Cold wet mud sat beneath her fingers. The air, nice and dry, filled her nostrils. She lay still. Alive. Waiting for her heart to slow, she examined the sky above. The dark clouds had cleared. Azure and white streaks remained. Peaceful. Almost bliss.

A laugh bubbled up from her nearly frozen lips. Why couldn't life be like that, bumpy, dreadful, and then all clear?

She sat up, limbs shaking. Now, both slippers were gone. Her big toe popped free from a hole in her stockings. The digit looked purple. If she didn't get warm, she would die.

Rubbing her foot, she scanned the landscape. A cottage sat off in the distance. Puffy grey smoke left its chimney. Could she get help there? What if darkness lived there?

Shivering, she tried to think of another option. She wouldn't make it back to Tomàs land or even the house. Not this time. There was no other option but this cottage and strangers.

With all her strength, she lifted and started toward the house.

The limestone brick looked familiar. It was the vicarage for Clanville. Old Reverend Playfair. He'd help. He helped everyone.

The old man knew everyone. He might know Sarah. Did the girl live?

Amora pressed toward the vicarage. Her toes tingled. Her fingers must have fallen off, for she felt nothing pounding upon the door.

A baby's cries sounded inside. Maybe the vicar was busy. Her head hurt. She could go no further. With all her might, she knocked again. This time the door opened.

A man holding a child stood in the threshold. His deep brown hair. Cheery smile. The way he held the babe swaddled in a green pinafore. It was familiar.

"Mrs. Norton?"

The vicar. The one who prayed for her during that awful night when she miscarried. The one who said he believed her. "Vi-car Wil…"

Her teeth chattered so badly she couldn't finish. She slumped against the threshold.

"Mrs. Norton, you're hurt. Come inside." He grabbed her about the waist and towed her into the vicarage.

Juggling the baby, he tugged her into the parlor and made her sit in front of the fireplace. "Mrs. Turnbill! Mrs. Turnbill!"

Stooping next to her, he scooted out of his jacket, and placed it about her shoulder. "Come on, Jack, the good woman needs a hug. Let's keep her warm."

Bundled in his jacket, she felt his hands rubbing her back. His warm breath cascaded her fingers.

A short plump woman maybe Mother's height poked her head into the room. "Yes, Reverend. Do you need... Oh, my."

"Mrs. Norton has had an accident." He massaged each of Amora's palms, splaying them against the carpet, pointing them toward the onyx iron grate of his firebox. "Get some blankets. Then fetch a doctor."

"Right away, sir." The woman threw up her hands and ran. The sound of pattering feet disappeared, eclipsed by the crackle of the fire.

"No doctor." Amora's fingers trembled in spite of the man's effort. The whitewashed walls and emerald sofa became blurry. She touched her face, but felt nothing.

Vicar Wilson craned his head to the door. "My housekeeper needs to hurry. You look--"

"Like a drowned rat?" She pushed at her hair. Locks fell everywhere. At least she was too cold to feel her cheeks darken.

"Far from it. Just cold. Very blue."

He set the boy down near her. The vicar took his fingers and rubbed her face. "You are very cold."

The little boy reached up and grabbed a fist full of her dripping locks.

"Jack, this is my friend, Mrs. Norton." He cooed at the baby, then turned back to her. "Did you get caught in the storm?"

She smiled at the baby, but her teeth rattled the truth. Blinking, she stared into the minister's walnut colored eyes and sank down onto the jute rug. With a thick tongue, she said, "You...y' believed me without proof."

Her eyes closed, and the only person to believe her drifted away.

Barrington tugged at his horse's reins. Another pass along the bank might reveal Amora. His pulse exploded within his veins. So close to saving her on the cliff, so close. Why couldn't he have gotten her away from the precipice before it crumbled? Why did she push him? They could've fallen together. He might have been able to free her from the undercurrents. Or they could've died together.

He cupped a hand over his eyes and scanned the river. Nothing. No raven hair. No floating body.

His spectacles fogged in the chilly air. He couldn't accept the sense of loss filling him. "God, don't take her from me. I have to make things right. Give me one more chance. Just one."

He brought the horse around again. The gelding obeyed without question. Barrington's moments of swaying in the saddle disappeared. My how all of his training returned. If only he'd been taught to be a better husband.

His father taught him nothing. The man married his mother, a wealthy shopkeeper's daughter just for her dowry when Grandfather cut him off. Though legally and lawfully wedded, his father never came home except between gambling excursions, never defended her from gossip or the subtle taunts of her black race, never loved her like she deserved.

The man rubbed his mother's nose in each of his scandals until Grandfather stepped in and dealt with the situation, banishing the ne'er-do-well to the continent. Grandfather ruled the family with an iron grip. The Norton name became respectable again, but managing under fear and little love didn't seem quite right either.

The clouds started to gather, blocking what little sun the day possessed. He needed help. If she survived the river, Amora would die of exposure. A larger search party was required. The old vicarage was over the next hill. He'd get them involved. For what it was worth, the whole of Clanville needed to find his precious girl.

Barrington jumped off the horse and ran up the short drive. Before he could knock, the door opened. An older woman ran past him. She turned and clutched at his coat. "You there. Get on your master's horse and ride to town and get the doctor. He's probably at the tavern."

He closed his eyes for a moment. He'd been away from Clanville so long, folks must've forgotten their mulatto neighbor. "Ma'am, I can't. I have an emergency. My wife fell into the river. I need to get people to come search for her. Can you run for help?"

Her light eyes widened. She clung more tightly to his coat. "Your wife? She's inside. Very poor shape. Vicar Wilson's with her."

She let go and took off down the path.

Barrington marched inside. "Wilson, Amora!"

"In here, Norton."

He followed the voice and found them in a parlor. Amora lay wrapped in a blanket, like a meat pie tucked in a browned crust. Wilson rubbed her blue fingers as a fire blazed. A little girl blew on the wool covered lump where toes should be. A small boy sat near her back pulling locks of her hair. The little family attempted to save his wife.

Dropping to the ground, Barrington whipped off his hat and gloves and mimicked the minister's action with Amora's other hand.

She was alive or maybe just barely. God gave him one more chance to make amends.

He cleared his throat. "How long has she been here? I've been scouring the woods."

Wilson stood up and paced. "Not long. My housekeeper took off her soaked gown and put her on one of my shirts. I don't know how to get her warmer." The man frowned. He must genuinely care.

"Heat. Body heat. A wounded soldier would die if his core didn't stay warmer than his extremities." Barrington scooped Amora up into his arms. "Is there a bedroom or chamber?"

The man rubbed his jaw. "Becky, keep Jackson safe. Come with me, Mr. Norton."

Amora lay still, almost lifeless within his arms. His poor girl. How could he still breathe with his heart outside of his ribs?

The vicar climbed up a steep flight of stairs, and then pushed open a door to a room on the right. Taking the candle from the sconce in the hall, he lit up a lantern on a table, then went to work on the fire.

Once a blaze roared, he plodded to the threshold. "I'll be outside waiting for the doctor." Wilson slammed the door.

Barrington laid Amora onto the mattress. Making quick work of his buttons, he thrust off his coat and shirt. Throwing each boot a different direction, he returned to her, picked her up, and crawled into the bed with her.

Digging beneath her wrapping, he freed her of the coarse shirt and tugged her tightly against his chest, molding her frail limbs against him. He rubbed her frozen skin until the delicate porcelain felt as warm as the woolen blanket. He let his breath heat her cheeks as he played with her fingers, working them from side to side to renew the blood flow. With his legs, he trapped her toes, coddling them, using friction to return her feet to life.

She was lovely and delicate. All his, always his. And his foolhardy quest for the truth made her want to die. What kind of love had he given her?

His hands curved about her abdomen, tucking her as close to him as possible. When she felt as warm as he, Barrington snuggled with her beneath the blankets. He hoped she knew he was there, believing in her, trying to save her life.

Chapter Four: Waiting for Amora to Awaken

Cravat flopping from hastily dressing, Barrington paced back and forth. He leaned from side to side against the wall outside of the bedroom where Amora fought for her life. His head ached as it kept spinning images of her falling, of her dying. He'd watched the love of his life slip into the water, and then disappear. She was lost to him in that moment.

He closed his palms. They were still raw as if they held her icy toes and fingers.

"Some tea, sir." Mrs. Turnbill, the vicar's housekeeper held a tray in front of him, her eye's focused on the tray. She must've realized he wasn't a servant.

The scent of chamomile and fresh biscuits wafted to his nose, but he couldn't eat. Amora wasn't, so he wouldn't. "No, thank you."

Hunger meant nothing right now. He'd stay alert on post until she awakened.

Mrs. Tomàs sat in a chair. Her gaze never left the dark stained door. She waved the housekeeper away as well. Her dark black eyes looked glassy.

He had no words of comfort to offer. Or blame. This was Barrington's fault.

Mrs. Turnbill withdrew, stopping only to whisper to Wilson as she passed him on the stairs.

The vicar tugged his arms behind his back. "Why don't you both come down and sit in the parlor? It's more comfortable. The doctor said he'd come for us once she awakens."

The man's tone sounded chipper. But how could the vicar be confident Amora would recover? He didn't count the seconds between her labored breaths. Nor did he feel the death chill emanating from her neck and bosom.

Barrington rubbed his face. The memory of her giving up came into focus, repeating each time he closed his eyes. Recovery had as much to do with attitude as it did the wound. Right now, his girl ached. She was in enough pain to jump off a cliff rather than be with him.

The vicar pivoted from Barrington to Mrs. Tomàs. "Please, ma'am, at least you."

Digging into her reticule, Mrs. Tomàs found a lacy handkerchief and wiped her eyes. "No, I need to be here. My daughter hates doctors and might be frightened when she awakens. Hopefully, she'll want her mother."

That wouldn't be likely. Barrington righted the buttons on his waistcoat. "I'll be here if she's confused."

Wilson stepped closer to Mrs. Tomàs's seat, folded his arms and leaned against the chair rail molding decorating the wall. "How did Mrs. Norton end up in the river?"

"She fell. The rain made the cliff unsteady. It was an accident."

Rubbing his jaw, Wilson looked up toward the

whitewashed ceiling. "This is sacred ground, Mr. Norton. It's good to tell the truth here."

"I don't lie. The cliff gave way. She shoved me so I wouldn't fall too."

"Why was she on the cliff in the middle of a storm?"

Barrington gazed at Mrs. Tomàs, but she picked at the edging of her handkerchief as she shifted within her chair.

"Fine. Hide things. Mrs. Norton told me before she fainted."

In two steps, Barrington overshadowed the man, crowding him against the wall. "What did she say?"

Wilson didn't flinch. He met Barrington's gaze. "You believed me without proof. That was her exact quote before she succumbed."

Barrington pulled back and dimmed his eyes.

"Is this your way of dealing with things? I told you your wife was in trouble. I convinced her to confide in you, and you didn't have the decency to believe her."

Dagger in his gut, sharp with the same accusations he'd told himself as he searched for Amora, he turned and put a hand on her door. "You are right, Wilson. I failed her. I failed."

He swallowed the self-pity forming in his soul. "I let her down, again. Is that what you want to hear too, Mrs. Tomàs?"

"It's not your fault." His mother-in-law's voice warbled. "I convinced her never to tell, but the truth always comes out."

"No one can bottle these memories up, not of something this traumatic." The cold clinical tone of Wilson's words twisted the dagger a little more. "She suffers from it every day, bottling it inside for your benefit."

Barrington wanted to put forth an excuse, some legal brief explaining how he got things so wrong, but even a lousy barrister, one without his skills knew a losing case. He slapped at his neck, pounding again his sentence. Guilty. Guilty of negligence, guilty of not seeing and believing the best girl in the world, guilty of withholding his love in fear of being made a fool.

The sounds of Wilson's low heels moved again, the slight pacing he'd done every hour on the hour. Anxiety lay beneath his calm exterior. He stopped and turned toward Barrington. "Though Mrs. Norton's been disappointed, I sense there is strength inside too. She walked a good distance to come to me."

Barrington looked upon the reverend's lean face trying hard to mask the agitation at some other man laying claims to Amora. "What do you mean?"

"She smiled at my son as she trembled. She sacrificed herself for you. The memories haven't robbed her of a sense of loving others."

Loving others. Barrington had thought it a flaw, Amora's needling him so much about working too much, needing to know his every whereabouts because of her fear of something happening to him. It wasn't a flaw but a mask of her symptoms of distress. Why hadn't he seen it?

"Mr. Norton," the vicar said, his voice steady and low, "She is strong, but everyone has weaknesses and can make wrong choices."

Amora, the girl he left before going to war, was very strong-willed. Witty and gifted, so different from the woman he married. Yet, the strength in Amora's voice as she remembered the Sarah person, another captive, surprised him. And only when Barrington offered to help find the girl did Amora stop fighting his help. Perhaps finding this woman could focus Amora on becoming well. "Vicar, how do you know so much about this?"

"I counseled a few women who suffered terrible abuses. The night of Mrs. Norton's miscarriage, I listened to her fevered delusions. I've heard similar stories. No one lies about things that dark."

Mrs. Tomàs snorted into her handkerchief. "What happened to the other girls?"

Wilson lowered his head and swiped at his brow. "Many couldn't endure the shame. Alienation made them make wrong choices."

Wrong choices. Barrington had made a series of wrong choices the past week, maybe the last five years. "I should've let you help." He stoked the panels of her door and wanted nothing more than to rush inside and hold her again. Everything needed to take second place to Amora. "I almost lost her today, could still lose her."

The knob turned, and the doctor stood in the threshold. "She's asking for you."

Barrington tugged at his cravat and marched forward, but the man held out a hand, blocking entrance.

Ale wafted from the doctor's breath and the pores upon his baldhead. The stench twitched Barrington's nose, reminding him of the tavern in town and the bushes out back, ones from which he'd dragged his intoxicated father. "Out of the way, sir. My wife is asking for me."

The doctor lifted a hand to him again. "Mrs. Norton's asking for the vicar."

Wilson peered at Barrington. "Do I have your permission to help Mrs. Norton?"

His fist balled beneath his tailcoat. Barrington took a deep breath. Pride, jealousy. None mattered, only his wife's health. He put a palm on the vicar's shoulder and nodded. "Whatever she needs, she'll have it."

"Good." Wilson trudged into the room and closed the door.

Barrington pounded one hand into the other. *God, let this be the right thing.*

Chapter Five: Needing an Ally

Amora opened her eyes as Vicar Wilson stepped into the stark white bedchamber. Her pulse raced as memories of being locked in the tiny chamber at Bath returned. Those vicious doctors.

She swallowed and forced moisture to her dry tongue. "Sir, I am *sor…*" Wiping her lips of the useless word, she started anew. "I hate that I have caused such an upset to your household."

A smile filled his cheery countenance. "River sprites are always welcome."

He plodded forward and put his hand along the smooth post of the headboard. "Instead of swimming in cold winter waters, you can come talk with me. Or you could give my Becky art lessons. Your mother says you're a good painter."

"A long time ago, I had talent." She shook her head. "When will Mr. Playfair be returning?"

His smile tightened. "The resurrection. My cousin passed last yuletide."

Her heart sank. Only Mr. Playfair knew everyone.

Now how could she find Sarah?

"Mrs. Norton, you can talk to me. I can be a confidant just like Playfair."

Feeling alone and confused, she let a renegade tear leak down her face. She rolled to her side before more came.

His footsteps sounded far away. She peered over her shoulder and watched him move toward the door. "I am going to let you rest."

She couldn't. She needed an ally, someone with whom she could reason her thoughts. That person wasn't a virtual stranger like Mr. Wilson or Barrington. "Wait."

"Yes, Mrs. Norton."

There was one person who now claimed to believe her. "Could you send my mother to me?"

The reverend nodded. "You can trust me, too." He slipped from the room.

As if she'd been shot out of a cannon, Mother ran through the threshold. "You wanted me, dear?"

Amora motioned her forward. Though still very beautiful, the woman had aged. Her fingers appeared thin and frail. More silver graced her dark chignon. Time kept moving, even if Amora didn't want it to.

Sitting up, she put her head against the walnut frame and tugged the bedclothes and blankets up to her chin. "Barrington said you believe me. Why? Why now?"

The lady eased onto the mattress. She pulled her shawl tight about her shoulders and balled the onyx knit fabric around her palms as if to hide her guilty hands. "I've believed you for a while now. Almost as soon as I got you home from Bath, but you'd stopped talking to anyone until Mr. Norton returned from the war. I should've told you then. I let my pride keep me from saying so."

"Then why did you tell Barrington?"

"Years without seeing you or your sister have given me plenty of time to think. I can't ignore my guilt of how I dealt with you. You never lied to me, and I let you be treated dreadfully. I would have never let those English butchers torture you, if I'd known what they'd do."

Amora's fingers almost clawed through the weave of the soft blue blanket. She took a breath. Her aching chest rattled from the effort. How could one be so cold and yet smolder with fury?

Her mother scooted close. The thick Mechlin lace adorning her sleeves billowed like sails. The woman held out her arms as if she wanted to hug her. The delicate lady with her tawny brown skin could play the role of a grieving widow better than any, but Amora wouldn't play along. "No more fake sentiment. None."

Her mother came closer, her jeweled hand outstretched. "Amora?"

Bracing for a slap, Amora tensed then forced her shoulders to relax. She wasn't that waif who crawled home for safety. No, just a woman who'd nearly killed herself and her husband. "I suppose this *proves* what a sorry sight I am."

Mother's fingers lifted Amora's chin. She splayed her pinkie in her crazy drooping locks. "My poor dear. A mad man held you captive. I know that now." She tugged her fully into an embrace. "Instead of welcoming you home, I let my pride imprison you all over again. I'm so sorry."

That word *sorry* made the air heavy. The hug felt soggy and stifling. Things weren't fixed because Mother wished it so. She pulled away.

Wiping at her eyes, Mama sat up straight. "I pray for you daily." Her proud voice cracked, almost whimpering. It sounded desperate, so like Amora's desperation. "I want Isis to make both of my daughters happy."

Mama and her idols. Amora sighed at the notion of praying to wood. Well, now at the whole notion of prayer. "I thought I could trust you now, but I'm not sure."

She picked up Amora's hand and brought it to her lips. "I believe you. Hear me. Know that this is real."

It was so hard to discern between what was true and what was falsehoods. "I want to. But did you shed tears, or pray to the wooden god when you learned of the doctors' treatments, the scalding hot baths, knocking me off tables, foul elixirs, which vomited out everything inside? Now nothing can grow inside. You and Papa's cousin let them kill my spirit, what little there was left."

Mother rubbed her stomach. "Barrington told me about your miscarriage."

She grabbed Amora in a tight embrace, pushing out the little air in her withered lungs. "I'm so sorry."

Amora closed her eyes. The complaints, the accusations had to all be out in the open. "I hate the pitiful sprite I've become. I won't be her anymore."

"Look at me. I've done wrong by you and by Barrington. I'll spend the rest of my life making amends. Please let us start anew. Let me be of help to you."

Tears puddled by Amora's nose. It had to be river water. How could she have any tears left in her eyes? How could she still weep over yesterday? Yesterday, a few months, a few years, all blended but overshadowed by the memory of this woman's voice shouting, *Wild like a mangy mutt. How dare you come back here with your tail between your legs! You're a disgrace to the Tomàs name."*

Strangling in her sobs, Amora pushed free. "I never betrayed Barrington, and yet my captor wouldn't kill me. Maybe he knew you and Barrington would later." She held her wrists out, one still bearing a nicely healed slit. "A thousand cuts with your disapproval."

"Amora, no!" Her accent, the one she'd worked so hard at removing came out. "I am so ashamed I let others hurt you. How do I make amends? Tell me. I'll do anything."

This was real. She touched Mama's wet cheeks, catching a few of the tears dribbling down her jaw. The salted water puddled in her thumb, and then ran down upon the veining of her palm. "You do hurt for me. But can I trust you again?"

"Ala mula y a la mujer, a palos se ha de vencer."

The sounds, the syllables and cadence of her mother's voice were perfect for Papa's favorite teasing phrase, *a mule and a woman can only be defeated by a stick*. For a moment, she could picture him standing at Mama's side, laughing with his big black gaucho cocked to the side of his head.

"I've been a mule, more so than a mother. Definitely not a woman of a compassion. The stick of truth has defeated me. I surrender. Let me humble myself to you."

Something deep inside Amora thawed. Her shoulders shook as a fresh wave of rawness erupted from her eyes. She couldn't breathe for crying so hard.

Mama stroked her face, lightly rubbed her temples. "I'll make it better if you let me. I won't let anyone hurt you again, not even me."

Counting to nine or nine hundred, Amora calmed and found herself in Mama's lap shrouded beneath her shawl.

"I love you, Amora. What can I do to prove it?"

Proof. "I'm sick of proof, Mama. Just show me. Don't let Barrington send me to Bath or Bedlam. No asylum. Promise me that."

Mother's brows knitted and her tresses flopped from her disheveled chignon and covered her eyes. "He wouldn't—"

"I didn't think you would either, but you did. Mama, I just waited on a high cliff hoping to fall off. He stood by me. I almost caused him to fall. He knows my thinking gets cloudy. Like the clients he's had put away. He'll do it to me too as if being locked in a tiny room with little light would make me better."

The images of the cellar, the asylum, of lost Sarah blended. There had to be freedom from this pain if she could find her friend. She wouldn't forget Sarah anymore. "Promise to stop him."

Mama drew her up against her bosom. The grip was tight. Maybe this time, she'd never let go.

"Take me to Tomàs Manor. This room is so small, so plain. It reminds me of Bath. I keep testing my arms to see if they are bound." She held the woman tighter, inhaling her comforting lavender scent. "Please let me be able to trust you again."

"I'll do all I can. And you'll be going nowhere but to Tomàs Manor, but Barrington is your husband. He does have the final word. It's his right."

"Maybe he shouldn't be my husband anymore."

"What? You love him. He loves you. He's outside pacing, waiting to see you."

His love wasn't enough. It didn't fill her emptiness or hide her from the memories. Now it just made her sad.

"I can't pretend I'm well around him anymore. I can't see him."

"The man hasn't left your door. Let him visit with you, just for a few moments."

"He almost fell off that cliff. He'll risk everything chasing after his crazed wife. Rumors of my behavior will get out. It will affect his career." That was first in his life, not Amora. She pushed away and crawled back under the blankets. "Lying to Barrington got me into this marriage. The truth should be able to free us. Find a way, something that will put me under your power since my judgment will always be in question."

"I'll try, Amora. It won't be easy. His mind is steeped in English law. If only I could get you back to Egypt."

"No leaving Papa's orchards. I'll get stronger feeling him about. Well, his good memories at least."

Amora lay back on the pillow and released a long breath. The word divorce stuck in her throat. Maybe saying it aloud would relieve the helplessness trapped in her lungs. The sentiment hurt as bad as the river's pressure. Freeing herself from Barrington's scrutiny and that of his London world had to be for the best. She pushed up as straight as her strengthless body could manage. "Help me divorce him."

"You want a d-divorce?" Mama stood and traipsed to the tiny window. She flicked the curtains betwixt her shaking palms.

"Concerned I'll be a blight to the Tomàs name? Father must be turning over in his grave at the thought of a Tomàs seeking divorcement. Maybe some pharaohs, too."

She came close again. "If that is what you want, Amora, I'll try to figure something out."

Mama was a force of nature. A typhoon when she wanted something. She could make the impossible happen. But could Amora trust that she'd fight for her?

As if she'd heard the doubts rattling in the cobwebs of Amora's skull, Mama sat on the bed and opened her arms wide. "I will never side against you again."

Taking a chance, Amora went into her embrace, sinking into arms that appeared to want her. "Make me one of your teas. Something that will put me to sleep. Let me awake in my old room. That way I won't have to say sorry for the hundredth time or witness pity in Barrington's face."

"Yes, dear." Her fingers combed through Amora's tresses. "Maybe I'll braid your hair, like old times. I'll put some honey in your tea. I know how you enjoy that."

Amora closed her eyes to a slit. Though she wished it never to happen, she had to stay vigilant to detect the moment Mama would betray her again.

Chapter Six: Past Yuletide

Standing at the window, Amora counted snowflakes, just the ones falling and melting against the glass. No running outside of Tomàs Manor to catch a perfect pattern on her tongue. If she did, the whole house would be in an uproar.

The six-week truce with her mother and Barrington would be over. Then what? Sent away by one of them. No snowflake was worth being put in an asylum. No, it was better to be fettered by imaginary chains than real iron locks.

She pulled at her shawl and looked outside again. Forty-two days had passed since she'd fallen into the river and nearly died, yet it wasn't enough time to regain her strength. She surely didn't have enough to pretend all was well.

Things weren't.

The nightmares were worse. They chilled her bones, robbed her of her sleep, so much more so than before. Mixed up voices of her lost friend, even acquaintances long dead, all filled her head when she closed her eyes.

Mama had been kind, waiting upon her, sitting with her until the lady's head nodded and tiredness overtook her. When Mama left, Amora would arise and paint. Feeling the brush betwixt her finger, the tart smell of the oils awoke a part of her that had been silent too long. Before she knew it, all her canvases were filled. Then those stark white walls had to vanish. Each stroke kept her mind from shredding to bits. Each smear of the horsehair bristles pushed aside the weight of the horrible images and sounds.

Thick iron links wrapped about her wrists.

The screams, the remembered moans of pure terror.

How many girls lost their dreams, their sanity because of the monster?

How long could she keep fighting before she couldn't?

She blinked in time to see a perfect snowflake land on the glass, flawless with its veining, its pristine color. Something to have caught on her tongue and pretend again that all was right.

That Barrington loved her.

In the silent hours of the night, the early mornings when she could no longer stand and had to lie down, that's when she needed him. Waking in his arms, listening to his heart thud in her ear always made it easier to remember that she'd escaped, that she was free. Now she had to depend upon handwritten notes with dates and little phrases for strength.

Yet, paper wasn't Barrington. It didn't possess a rumbling laughter, nor questions or accusations or pity. She leaned against the glass and let the chilly pane freeze her cheek. It had been a good two weeks since he gave up knocking on her door.

But he wasn't the kind of man to be easily deterred.

He must be biding his time, probably waiting for her fears to drive her back into his arms.

Dipping into her pocket, she pulled out one of her notes. One cut of twisted foolscap held the date. Another said she was free. All the proof she needed since she couldn't depend on Barrington.

Mama's voice carried down the hall. Probably instructing the cook on apple pie making or a maid on the proper way to dust her idols. Her mother prayed to the statue of Isis almost everyday. Did the polish mahogany figure hear her?

Probably not. Nothing had changed. Neither Barrington nor the ghastly memories had left.

Yet, her mother bore this time well. She even let the yuletide pass with no decorations or showy dinners — so against everything in the woman's nature.

No matter how much the woman claimed she'd stand by her, Barrington was her husband. He had all the power. An aggressive barrister couldn't be stopped.

Before fear or pity or her mother could come to her, she stepped out onto the portico. Closing the door behind her, she panted and let the crisp air work its magic. She slumped against the rail and looked out at the white lawn, the cream dollops of snow on tree branches. Papa loved this time of year, second only to harvest time. *Dear Papa, send me strength. I don't know what to do.*

"I like this time of year in Clanville. Everything so beautiful and snowy." The deep voice rose above her swirling thoughts. Barrington was here, not in the guest chambers reading. Why couldn't this one time, he be a figment of her imagination?

Caught like a rat in a trap, she whirled around to spy

him sitting in a chair bundled in his greatcoat, gloves, and top hat. Was he contemplating leaving?

No carriage was near.

Maybe he too wanted air. Maybe he wanted to be free and just couldn't force himself to say the words.

"Amora, you look well. Are you feeling better?"

"A little."

The front spindles of his chair were off the ground as it leaned against the wall. The thing teetered as if it would dump him to the ground. If it did, he'd hurt his hip. She raised a hand to caution him, then lowered it. He could take care of himself. "I'll leave you to your privacy." She turned to re-enter the house.

"Please don't go."

"Barrington, I've been out here too long."

"You mean you've been around me too long, a whole minute."

His countenance wore a painted smile. She remembered when his face lit with laughter. A slight dimple would appear at the corner of his lips. Right now, he seemed almost pained.

Backing up against the corner column, she folded her arms over her bosom to protect her heart from whatever he would say. Her arms trembled against each other. She hoped he couldn't see how vulnerable she was to his opinions.

She bit her lip and feigned calm. "I'll stand here another minute."

She caught his half-smile, but braced for his censure. Yet nothing came, just silence and stares.

Her minute stretched a little longer. The sun set around them. Shades of orange fell upon the lightly dusted portico. The colors even reflected in his spectacles. His eyes looked so sad. She'd put that pain there. Her heart whimpered. When would they stop hurting each other?

Counting to at least five hundred, she released a rattled breath as she started to the door. "Now, I'm beginning to tire. Goodnight, Barrington."

"Well, I should be grateful for the crumbs you've shown me."

She pivoted at the threshold. Knowing he was baiting her for a response did nothing to caution her. "What?"

"I need you to hear me out. I want you to forgive me."

With the hard edge in his voice, he'd give chase if she ran, so she stopped. Her short heels thudded atop the floorboards. "I don't want to argue or listen to your well thought out court statements. I'm not Justice Burns."

He released a deep sigh. "At least then I'd get a fair hearing. Well, let's talk about the cliff."

She'd rather listen to his apology. She tugged at her shawl. "What should I testify to? Do you want your lunatic wife to verbalize her desperation? I'm better. No need for you to be concerned. I'll pretend nothing has changed. You have my statement. Do with it what you will."

"I am concerned, Amora. I want to help."

He said the words so matter-of-factly, like they were discussing the weather. He must wonder if she'd make another attempt to jump. Who knows? She hadn't felt that low in a long time. Maybe she should be put into care. She raised her palms high. "I surrender to an official of the court. Just tell me what asylum you'll send me to for *help*."

His stare swept over her, making her cold fingers hot.

"Send you where? You'll go no place without me." He scratched at his chin, his tone softened. "Together, we should go to Cornwall. Remember the blue water and how happy we were. Some waves might not be frozen."

"Stop it. We'd never have gone there for a wedding trip if I'd told you the truth. We should never have married."

He cleaned his lenses and reared forward, planting his boots upon the creaking plank. "I loved you when we said our vows. I love you more so now that I know the truth, understanding what you endured. Let's go from here and start anew."

This was one of the main reasons why she'd avoided him. He'd say something noble, some lie her weak heart wanted to believe. She shook her head to the fib. "Tricks are beneath you. I'll go willingly this time to the asylum. Crazy people need to be put away where they can't hurt you, Mama, or anyone else."

"You're not crazed. Anyone can have a moment of despair."

"A moment?" Chuckles poured out of her mouth as tears taunted her eyes. "My moment nearly killed you, and we both know what my panic did."

She pressed at her abdomen as if her finger could wipe the guilt from her body, the agony from her soul. "Make this easier for me. Will it be Bedlam this time or the butchers in Bath?"

He wrenched at his neck, unfastening the top button on his greatcoat. "I'll not abandon you. Not again, not when you need me."

"Even the great Barrington Norton can't help." She shook her head and looked down at her low boots. "Just go love Cynthia or someone else. I want you happy. That can't be with me.""

"Amora, have you grown to hate me? Is there nothing in your heart for me?"

She gazed at him again, wondering why he was toying with her. She wasn't fit to be his helpmate, a position she'd lied to become. And why did he sound hurt? More tricks to make her think they could be happy. Never. Five years too late. "You'll do better in your career without me. I'll never be an asset. My temperament's not suited for politicking, and you can't be all you wish to be with an otherworldly wife."

His forehead wrinkled and settled into a deep frown. "I've been away from the courts for over a month. London is still standing. Well, it's been pre-occupied with the passing of George III."

"The king has passed, the one with mental distress?"

Barrington lowered his head as if acknowledging such would be an indictment against her. Did he assume all crazed people shared a bond? "That is sad to hear. He suffered a long time."

"Amora, London doesn't need me, but you do. My career means nothing without you."

"Aren't there bills to be paid? You must have saved a great deal without my candle expense. But no income for over a month, that has to be devastating."

He thinned his lips to a line and looked to the left. "I've used my inheritance. I'll use more if we need to be here longer."

Hadn't he vowed to make his own way? Stunned, she slouched against the column. Though his grandfather's influence was everywhere, Barrington kept the Norton family home, the great house adjoining Tomàs land, closed up. He only leased his grandfather's residence in

Mayfair to appease her mother's notion of a proper place to live. "This must be killing you to depend upon Old Man Norton's wealth."

He lifted from his chair and reached out, motioning her to come to him. "I'll do whatever it takes to make things right between us."

She shook her head and refused to move. If she stood too close, the hurt in his grey eyes would grab her, imprisoning her again in that place of needing him. Her heart could never be vulnerable to his opinions. Not again and stay well.

His fingers stroked the air then dropped away. "Amora, I love you. Someday, you'll know that again. If you don't want to go to Cornwall, we should leave for London."

Mouth twitching with silent screams of *no*, she locked her knees, clicking her heels again into the floorboards. "I don't want to go back, ever."

"You don't want to return?" His baritone faltered. "How long do you intend to stay here?"

How to tell him *forever*? Her lips couldn't form the words. Her forehead felt sticky as a breeze kissed her with a fresh dusting of snow.

"We used to be good at talking and a whole lot of other things." His gaze tangled with hers, then seemed to wrap about her, stroking her cheek, slipping the length of her neck.

Heat filled her face. The memories of him being everything for her still lived. She still wanted his touch, wanted to be wrapped up in him, but that part of her should've drowned in the river.

Stretching the shawl tighter around her shoulders, she gazed at the doorway and lifted her chin to the warm glow of the candles beaming through the windows. "I need to figure things out alone. And I don't do well in London."

"Things will be different. I'll be in early, no later than eight or nine thirty. I'll make you secure in my affections." He took a few steps closer and posted himself in front of the threshold, blocking her escape back into the house. "God has given me a great deal of clarity these past weeks. I will do so much better."

She noticed shadows under his eyes. His chin bore stubble. He seemed tired and sad, so different from the unflappable man she'd come to depend upon.

"Amora, I haven't been available for you, not enough. I'll change that." As if he moved in thick syrup, he plodded forward then stopped inches from her. "Maybe someday you'll believe in me once more."

Though her husband stood close, saying nice things, a wall remained between them. To cross it would be to admit needing him, to become that loathsome creature who hung on his every word, waited for his approval, and lived each day in fear of his love disappearing. "I can't depend on you. I don't like who I am when I need you."

He took another step. "We should be alone together to figure things out."

This near, she could see a softness, an uncertainty in his silvery eyes. She hadn't witnessed that in years. The smell of his skin, rich bergamot, permeated the air caressing her. For one second, she wanted those arms he held at bay to hold her tight.

Nonetheless, the minute she reached for him, he'd disappear. He'd find someone else who needed him more. Her lack of memories would be counted as lies.

She ended the trance and sidestepped him. "I can't do this anymore. I want a divorce."

Barrington stood back as if she'd slapped him. The wariness in Amora's eyes did the same damage. His horrible quest for the truth made her want to end their marriage. She hated him.

Well, he didn't like himself so much now either. Not believing her was a debt he had no idea of how to pay, but leaving her was something he couldn't do. "No divorce."

"Why won't you let me be? This must be miserable for you."

Was it possible for her frown to become bigger? Taking his spectacles from his face, he siphoned a deep breath. "Ask me to cut off a limb, do some great feat of strength, but not divorcement."

Shielding herself with her shawl, she looked at the floor planks, then tugged on the dark ribbons circling her bodice. Her gaze lifted and shot violet darts at his heart. "Your career will do better without me. Imagine the parties you can attend without fetching your sick wife."

He chuckled and righted his glasses. "Well, I'm sure since I fought with my patroness's son at her ball, my invitation list is small. The hothead mulatto doesn't make a good guest."

"Win another big case for the crown. You'll be forgiven."

He wiped at his mouth, marveling at how she thought everything was about his reputation. Yet, hadn't he stressed that, with every complaint about attending balls and parties or his work schedule? "I've made mistakes. And how many will seek my representation when I have virtually disappeared from London?"

The lower part of her lip trembled. "My fault. I know."

"It's not. My career is immaterial. Only you matter. How can we not be together?" He moved his arm to place his hand on the pole behind her head. She flinched, but he didn't withdraw.

She tapped her foot. Her shoes matched the fabric and pattern of the indeterminate color of her walking gown. Her mother's handiwork and so was this talk of divorce.

"You're not listening. I want a divorce. We each need to be free."

"You're not listening. I won't be away from you. And since I haven't bedded your sister or your mother, the courts won't grant one. You're the only Tomàs I desire."

Her cheeks darkened. Perhaps some small part of her wasn't immune to him.

He slipped off a glove and put a hand to her cold face. "From the moment I spotted you painting in the orchard, you've had my love. Nearly losing you has brought it all back."

Glassy violet eyes peered up at him, but no words. She stepped away. The lacy silk of her dress hugged her sleek neck, her rounded hips and slim bosom. The setting sun bathed her satin skin. How could this delicate girl have withstood the abduction only to be driven to suicide by his careless tongue?

"You are smart, Barrington. You could find a way to get one if you wanted."

"I will do nothing of the sort. You know me, Amora. Can't you tell how it hurts not being alone with you, not being able to touch you? I was going to take a walk, but couldn't bear missing the chance you'd ask for me. Ask for me, Amora. Let me back inside your world."

She glanced down at her feet. One foot covered the other.

He'd never been this passive or tentative in his life. Maybe his lack of surety fed her fears. He put his arms about her shoulders. He made the touch soft, to give her the freedom to flee. "You have every reason to think ill of me, but I want to begin anew. Let me earn your trust. I won't fail you."

She didn't look up, but her fingers played with a brass button on his greatcoat. She sometimes did that with his waistcoat when they danced or he held her. Maybe there was hope for him inside her stubborn head.

With a quickened breath, he drew her against him and massaged circles along her back. "I know it's going to take time to repair the damage I've caused. Believe me, nothing in my life is more important."

Never wanting their embrace to end, he stood there, holding her sculpting her curves to him. A tiny bit of lilac floated to him. That was her scent, the fragrance upon her neck when he first took her lips. The aroma of her bed sheets when they were of one accord. The memories of her smiles, her jubilant laughter pressed on his chest. Had she grown immune to this feeling?

His breath caught when she put a hand against his ribs, but she used the leverage to push away. "I won't let you sway me. I can't be vulnerable to you ever again. Your wishes, your needs are second to everything that doesn't concern me staying well. My opinions are first."

Her bosom heaved as if he'd kissed her. He should have and removed all this talk of numbers. "You and I are one. We are halves of the same heart."

"No. You have to be equals for that."

Her mind was set, fiery like the miracle who first fell in love with him in the orchards.

But so was his. "Amora, we cannot divorce."

"Mama thought you'd say that. So she's having her solicitor draw up her settlement for a separation, a church divorce instead of a parliamentary one."

Hadn't Mrs. Tomàs had enough meddling? Who knew what the kindly vicar whispered in Amora's ear? He visited with her twice this past week. "Your mother has thought of everything. To be clear, this is advice from the same woman who told you to lie to me. The woman who let you be put away."

Amora's mouth button closed. She dipped her head.

Perhaps he shouldn't have said that, but Amora found room in her heart to forgive her mother. Was his crime so worse? He looked overhead at the white land, the snow covered trees. Though he'd come to like Tomàs Manor more and more these past weeks, it was too close to the cliff where Amora fell. And how could she not stand here on the portico without remembering his biting words, *doesn't prove Amora was abducted?*

If he could get her away to London, he might be able to sway her. "Seems we are at an impasse for I won't abandon you like my father did my mother. You know... well, you should know me better than that."

"I want you happy, Barrington. Living like this, careful of your words, keeping my schedule, it made you unhappy. You can't constrain a man like you. You want success. You feel you have so much to prove. And maybe you do for your race. No one's worried about the capabilities of a half-Egyptian, half-Spanish, half-sane woman. Well, there is that one expectation of a woman not being barren, but I've reconciled to that failing."

He put a hand over his mouth to make sure his jaw wouldn't drop to the floorboards. Yes, being a mulatto meant proving he was two times better than the other barristers. Yes, he understood that the gentry or ton saw his dark skin before his dogged skills. But that driven spirit was what made him the man he was. "My career is important, but all the things you've numbered are second place to you. Don't you know that?"

"Intentions don't count anymore. Wishing things were different only frustrates the soul."

He pushed at his hat wanting to fan the frustration steaming in his cold breath. "Come away with me, Amora. I can't leave you here. I can't be without you, wondering what you're doing, fearing--"

"See, you have all these fancy sentiments." Her words came out slowly, but her luminous eyes burned with determination. "But living with a loon is a lousy bargain."

"You're not a loon. You've just been hurt."

"Hurt." She spun away wiping her countenance with her shawl.

The last thing he wanted was to make her cry. He wrenched open his coat for a handkerchief and fought the urge to pull her back into his arms. He yanked the lawn cloth free and handed it to her. "We lived with secrets for five years. Why don't we try living with the truth? Return with me to London, and let's work on our marriage in the light."

She sniffed and dabbed at her eyes. "London is for you. Go be the barrister that's the talk of the town for his legal skills, not his scandalous wife."

Since she seemed to care more about his career than

he did, maybe he'd use that to compel her. "If you are determined to part from me, I'll have nothing left but my profession. Your presence will quiet down rumors, salvaging my reputation. The fight with Charleton and my long absence must have it in ruins."

"You need me, Barrington?"

"Yes." Oh, how he needed her. For five years, they'd barely slept apart. In just a month's time, he didn't realize how many times he'd turned in bed expecting her there. "Yes. Only you can fix this."

"I never thought about you needing me."

There was something in her voice, a lilt of something unexpected. And whatever it was, it made his insides warm with hope. "Let's go back and squelch the rumors. It may take the upcoming season to put everything back in order."

"Another year of suffering is out of the question."

He felt his mouth twinge at her comparison of their marriage to suffering, but even her considering the option was an opportunity. Beggars couldn't be particular. It was an opening negotiation. He tapped his chest to come up with a reasonable number. "Two, two months then."

She turned to him, her eyes large. Was she desperate for another excuse?

"Mother can come with us? I won't do without her."

"Yes and your friend, the vicar can visit if he's in town." As if Barrington could stop either from sharing her attention. He released a pent up breath. "Do we have an understanding?"

She pulled at the beading of her neckline. "I don't want to pretend even for a day that all is well between us. No sharing quarters or husbandly expectations. No more of it."

It hit his gut hard stinging every bit of his pride, how much she distrusted him, how much she regretted their intimacy. "I'll sleep in my office like when I'm working, or my chambers down the hall, just like I've done at Tomàs Manor, unless…"

"Unless what?"

"You invite me." He let a chuckle fall hoping to cut through the tension thick between them. "I suppose that won't happen. You seem very convinced in wanting to separate. Yet, I'll try to be very dapper and appealing."

She rubbed her eyes. "Mayfair's not that comfortable. Tomàs Manor is warm with colors. The cold town house won't be a good distraction."

Grandfather's Mayfair with its pristine walls, wasn't it perfect? He tugged on his lapels, flapping the folds of his greatcoat attempting to come up with something to thwart this objection. Nothing.

Desperate, he clenched his teeth. "Decorate, paint a rainbow, but complete whatever project you start, even if it takes longer than our deadline to finish."

Barrington fixed his feet and tensed his stance, steadying himself as Grandfather turned within the Clanville Norton crypt at such an audacious request.

Yet, if wall paint distracted her and warmed up their home, it had to be for the best. He whipped off his glove and spread his palm wide. "Agreed?"

"This isn't dickering for a horse." She lowered her head. "Why can't you make this easy? You say you love me. If that's true, let me go."

He moved to her and jerked her into his embrace. "I'm not that big of a man. My world is crumbling at the thought of losing you. Every time I shut my eyes, you fall off that cliff, and my heart is ripped out anew."

With his thumb, he traced her jaw. "I need the feel of you to erase the deathly chill I absorbed from your skin as you clung to life. It seems like I've lost you twice, and you want me to give you up a third time."

"I don't feel so well. I need to lie down." She pressed at his lapel, but nothing on this earth could steal her from him, not again.

He lifted her feet from the floorboards, tucking her head against his shoulder, folding her into his greatcoat. "I'll take you to your room."

Before a protest could leave her pursed lips, he charged inside, up the stairs to her bedchamber. Kicking open the door, he trudged inside and laid Amora upon the mattress.

His own breath came in rapids spurts.

Her eyes were wide. Her gaze never left him. "Leave me to rest."

"Should I get you something, maybe a wet rag for your forehead?"

"No."

His pulse raced as he sat on the bed beside her staring at the lips he wanted to caress, at arms that should be about his neck holding onto him, fighting to restore their love.

But those arms never reached for him.

"Good night, Barrington."

So beautiful, yet so distant. She turned her head and stared at the wall as if she were alone.

It hit him right in his chest, cutting through a rib or three, the ones guarding his heart. His notion of fighting for their marriage made her miserable. He didn't want her to suffer any more.

Barrington stood and tugged off his greatcoat, slapping it over his shoulder. His gaze caught on a mural covering one wall and half the next. The scent of fresh oil paint teased his nose. Amora's work? Is this what she had done the last month?

The skill and beauty, it had to be hers. She'd painted a river flowing into a crowded city. Two tiny figures, no bigger than his thumb sat huddled together in the middle of the hustling scene. One of the young ladies had light colored hair, the other raven. The looks on the characters' faces, such loneliness. Is that how Amora viewed the world?

What remained of his heart, his will shriveled. He wasn't a comfort, but part of the coldness she'd painted, maybe one of the busy people, ignoring the ladies' plight. He swallowed hard. How on earth could he win Amora's trust? Was this nothing more than a fool's errand?

He touched the wall, circling the lost women. "I know what we will do these next two months. I'm going to solve this crime. I will find your abductor."

Amora's head whipped around in his direction. Her eyes shone like wet stones freshly polished on a lapping wheel. "You think it's possible to find the culprit now?"

The notion of justice caught her interest. This was the opening he needed to win this case. "God made me a barrister, a very good one. The fiend will pay and that will restore your peace. I don't care how old the crime. With my tenacity and your memories, we can do this together, but I need your help to do it."

She put her fingertips to her temples, tapping. "The stuff in here is jumbled. What if I tell you I heard your friend Gerald Miller's voice while I was locked in that pit, the man you said died in the war saving your life.

Will you believe my memories then?"

The foolishness, which Cynthia talked about of her brother being alive buzzed in his ear like a nasty fruit fly. Amora had a reason to be mistaken whilst under such torment, not Miller's sister.

He pushed at his brow and pondered the most delicate way to correct his wife and not sound skeptical. There was none. "Miller is dead, but it could be a man who sounded very much like him. We have plenty to investigate."

"We?"

"Yes, I am serious about figuring this out. I've taken the time here to do some research. When I spoke with the magistrate, he mentioned Miller's particular friend, one named Druby, a Nan Druby. She was found about the time you escaped."

"She's dead, isn't she?" Amora's face blanked, her cheek twitched. She must remember the milkmaid.

His gut stung anew. "Yes." He should've asked directly if Amora had witnessed the cruelty inflicted upon the girl, but from the sudden paleness of his wife's skin, the stretching of her pupils - all indicated she had. "But I've found nothing yet on a Sarah."

She twisted her hands and drew her knees to her chin. "No, Sarah. I guess I was lying. Once a liar, always—"

"Your Sarah might have come down from one of the surrounding towns or even London, passing through Clanville when she too was abducted. That would account for no reports of her being missing."

Please see how seriously I'm taking this upon me. He folded his arms to keep them from exposing his angst. She needed to believe in him one more time.

"Down from London." She nodded and seemed to

mouth Sarah's name.

"Whilst we were still in London, I'd been looking into abductions since Smith, the man I left you… I convicted him of coining, but he confessed to being a party of this worse crime. I am sure once we are back in London, I could gather resources and quickly find all the Sarah's who might have been missing about the time of your abduction. But only you could identify her. I will need you.

With her brow scrunching, Amora counted her fingers. Had he offered her enough so that her scales balanced in Barrington's direction?

She looked up, her violet eyes filled with questions. "You've been looking for Sarah. Don't you need more proof of her existence than just my words?"

He'd discover a molehill miles away if that gave Amora a chance not to hate him. "There are villains out there who've hurt and killed women. They must be found and made to pay. Amora, someone hurt you, took away your zeal. For that reason alone, I will not stop until I catch him. You know me. I will find your villain and he will be executed."

"So you will search for every monster from Clanville to London. You will be busy."

"That's why I need you, to prioritize my steps. Only you can identify Sarah."

The Dark Walk abductions in London and Amora's, could they be related? A similar villain. A shudder raced up his spine, but he shoved that thought to the recesses of his mind and returned to his goal of getting his wife to willingly work with him to find her fiend. "Together, we can find your monster and *your Sarah*, but it can only be accomplished with your help. I need all of you, your spirit and your heart to put the pieces together."

Amora folded her arms about her legs and looked away. "I'll try for two months if you are serious about letting me help."

"If I give you my word, you can count upon it. We'll leave in the morn."

He slipped out of the room before she had a chance to change her mind. Heart thundering with desperation, he leaned against her closed door. Solving an old crime was nearly as impossible and almost as hard as finding a person gone five years. Yet, if those miracles gave his wife hope and a little piece of her soul back, then Barrington would move heaven and hell to give her those reasons to live.

Chapter Seven: An Honest Hurt

Amora smoothed her dark scarlet almost-black colored skirts as she sat opposite her husband at a table in the Prospect of Whitby. A tavern. She was at a tavern. She'd never been to such a lively place in London, or any other. The stench of spilt ale and sweaty working men filled the room, making her senses swim.

It had been a gale-forced rush getting back to London. As if he had a timepiece counting each minute, Barrington hurried and cajoled her mother to pack. Getting them back to London and settled in Mayfair in less than a day was an amazing feat with all of mother's trappings.

Amora thought she'd get a week to rest before Barrington acted on his promise. Instead, he shocked her, sending a mid-morning note drafted from the Old Bailey's. He requested that she be ready for an evening outing. Mama and her maid had to hurry their stitching, making this older dress from her treasured trunk in the attic like new. With full mourning still occurring in London, it was the most color she could manage and not indict the couple as heretics.

Something inside Amora dizzied at the attention. Yet, husband and wife sat in a public house, barely speaking to each other. In fact, Barrington seemed quite bothered.

A drunk staggered in. "Welcome to Devil's Tavern." He waved his hands to a group of fellows huddled in the back.

She looked over at Barrington. He looked uncomfortable with his nose wriggling beneath his silver frames. "I thought you said this was Whitby."

He plucked off his spectacles, and fiddled with the eyewear's limbs. "It's Whitby now. Old fools call it by its former infamous moniker."

"Why are we here? It will be dark soon. I don't want to be out too late."

His lips pressed together as he shoved his lenses back onto his face. "The magistrate gave me a name, Sarah Jenkins."

Sarah Jenkins. Amora's stomach flopped, but one whiff of the lavender-scented handkerchief mother gave her made it settle. The woman made her special teas to build her strength. She had been true to her word. Maybe she could be trusted.

"This could be your Sarah. We'll know soon."

"Could it be Sarah? Was it that simple, just asking for your help?"

His eye's distant gaze settled on her. There was something there. It wasn't quite pain, like when his hip ached, but there was a glimmer of it. Had he hurt himself at court today?

He looked away, scanning the room from side to side. He'd never seemed so flustered. "We'll know soon enough."

"Barrington, are you well?"

He swiped at his forehead. "I don't like taverns. I spent far too much time in these pulling my father out of them. Bad mem…"

His lips clamped for a moment. "I'm one to talk about dark memories. Yours are more atrocious."

"It's no competition. You don't talk that much of him, only of your grandfather."

His fingers drummed the table and just when she thought he'd give no response, his lips moved. "It was difficult growing up beneath his drunken shadow and grandfather's severe one. To this day, the smell of these places, the careless one's of the bushes outside, they offer nothing but unease."

In all their years, these few sentences were the most Barrington had ever said of his father. She latched onto his gaze and stared at him. "What was it about your mother that attracted him?"

"Her money. He'd been widowed a year and burnt up all his late wife's money. Grandfather had cut him off to set him straight. So my father picked a woman with a large dowry, but he made his choice hoping to offend Grandfather's notions of a proper bride. That made my mother, a free black heiress, the perfect option."

He seemed to wince with each carefully chosen word. "Was there no love?"

"She loved him. He loved brandy. Not a good match. When she became very ill, grandfather stepped in, took care of us until her passing. Why these questions?"

"I've always wondered, but didn't think I could ask."

His lip twitched. "Yes, I suppose you have nothing to lose in asking now, and it's not like I have a choice in avoiding these questions. Couldn't let my reticence offer another reason to decide against me."

Her eyes popped wide at the rawness of his voice. "I don't mean to put you in such a position, especially since you've kept your word about finding Sarah."

He nodded and lightly drummed the table. His strong shoulders sagged under his weighty greatcoat. "I said that I would find her. I have to make some of my promises to you true. The others, let's call them vows, are up for interpretation."

She peeked at him from between her lashes. It was one of his funny rebukes, but she didn't care. Pride and a smidge of warmth swam inside. In spite of his workload, this was a priority to him. She was a priority.

When she offered him a smile, he looked away, fumbling with the gold pin clasped to his cravat. Was he nervous? Was there something he wasn't telling her? "What did the magistrate say to make you think this is my Sarah?"

"The magistrate said this Sarah Jenkins disappeared in July, 1813. That was a month before your father died, a short period of time before you…were abducted." His breathing seemed to slow, if not stop.

"You can say the word to me, Barrington. I'm not that fragile." Well, not any more than the average loon."

He cleared his throat and then rotated his neck from left to right again, searching like the monster would come and grab her off the seat. What else did Barrington know and just chose to omit? "Did he say more? A simple date is not *enough proof*."

Leaning over the table, he thumbed his chin. "The father stated she was held in a dark place. It could be the same as where you were kept. Only you can tell me if it's your Sarah.

He fidgeted, then sank back into the hard chair. "My solicitor, Mr. Beakes, located this woman right away. He verified that this barmaid was the same Sarah Jenkins mentioned in the complaint."

Her stomach churned, switching from pride of the well-connected barrister to utter frustration. He chose his words too neatly. Barrington knew something he felt she was obviously too weak to comprehend.

"People can change a great deal in five years. Take a good look. Everything can become different the more time that passes."

Was he talking about Sarah or their marriage? A lump worked its way into her throat, but she wouldn't be deterred in hoping for her friend. "You were right to come back to London."

"Even I can get lucky sometimes." A sigh seeped out of him. "I pray this is your Sarah. I'd like to think I've done something that matters for you."

What was wrong with Barrington? His odd tone stabbed at her heart. Pity she had nothing inside to offer for comfort. Until she could put the pieces of her life back together, she couldn't be of use to him or anyone else.

Her husband's head whipped toward a harsh clink of mugs. His knuckles grew tighter as he gripped the table. "I forgot how loud these places were."

"What?"

"The tavern by the smithy in Clanville. It's not quite as big as this, but it's just as loud on the days the wages get distributed. My father would sit in the darkest corner away from the door. He said it was easier to see him coming."

She couldn't take her eyes from Barrington, captivated

by the unease creasing his countenance. "Who could he see coming?"

He straightened as if her question drew him from a trance. "My grandfather. He used to find him, settle his tab, and then attempt to walk off the stupor. When I got older, it was my job."

Blam! The sound of a man's fist connecting with the face of another as he punched him a few feet from their table. The man landed with a loud whack. The row continued with shoving and foul insults until the fellows brawled outside the window by her seat.

She almost put her hands to her ears as whispered curses from the monster filled her brain, but one look at Barrington's grimace froze her limbs.

The tense press of his lips spelled trouble or, more so, regret. "I'm sorry, Amora."

Sorry was a despicable word. His lips formed the *s* again. Her insides churned.

"Sorry about this. I got so excited about getting you a name, I didn't think of the risks. I'm not doing a very good job of protecting you."

She wanted to put him at ease, but what if he twisted her words and thought her too weak to help in the hunt? She lowered her palms to the table, tracing a long scar deep in the worn oak surface. "It's fine. We need to find Sarah. Her memories may be more reliable. The three of us will be able to find the culprit. You'll get another win for your court record."

"Perhaps, but it's more important to me for you to win." He reached across the rough wood, his fingers almost touching hers, but she drew her hands down into her lap.

Finding Sarah didn't change things between them.

She'd always be weak and otherworldly to him. After they found Sarah and even the abductor, Barrington wouldn't need her.

Other than sharing her bed, when had he?

A blonde buxom woman in a tight tunic sauntered to their table. Her bright blue eyes beamed as her hips pitched with each step. A wide mahogany tray balanced upon her arm. "Mr. Cardon said ye wanted to speak with me."

Barrington took a guinea from his pocket. He spun it then covered it with his palm. "We have a few questions for you to answer. This is yours if you are helpful."

The woman laughed. A whistle fled her flared nostrils. "Anythin' ye say mister. Anythin' you need, too."

The look of her was coarse. Her bosoms nearly fell out of her stained tunic. Had Sarah changed so much? The hair seemed right, but this girl was vulgar. Her Sarah wasn't, was she?

Amora scratched her temple. "Do you remember me?"

"From what? I can vouch for ye if the price is right. Especially if Mr. Tense can save me from the judges."

The tone of the woman and her familiarity with Barrington didn't sit well. It made her nauseated. "You know my husband?"

The barmaid reached over and settled her hand along Barrington's lapel. "The reputation of one of Bailey's finest and I mean fine as a good'n. You saved a friend from jail. She didn't pinch her 'mployer's silver. Ye proved it on the stand. He's a good black."

Barrington brushed off her hand then scooped up the coin. "We need answers. Tell us about the time you were abducted."

Sarah started laughing. Her low bodice shook, giving quite a show. The saucy maid popped over to Barrington again. "'Twas no abduction. I lied to keep my pappy from killin' me."

The air rushed out of Amora's lungs. She lowered her face toward the table and counted more scratches, anything to avoid Barrington's glare.

"So you weren't abducted?" His voice sounded smooth, controlled, but his fingers tapped. "You allowed your father to make a false complaint to the magistrate? He claimed you were taken by the Dark Walk Abductor."

"Ya. I didn't mean no harm. And no one was findin' those girls anyway. I just repeated the rumors — a dark room, chains."

The callousness of the barmaid burned. How dare she. "If you lied, how will anyone believe those who were actually taken? Why would anyone believe me?"

The barmaid leaned close to her ear. The large girl's shadow blocked the dim light from the tallow candles rimming the room. "Mr. Tense over there looks like 'e'll throttle the likes of ye. No wonda ye fibbed."

Amora sought her husband's face. Tense wasn't the word for the tightness in his jaw. It could be described as pained beyond measure like when his grandfather passed three years ago. Her heart sank.

Barrington shoved his fists under the table. "Miss, just tell my wife why."

"My fath'r had a temper. And I couldn't let 'im know his daughter was wanton." She pivoted to Barrington, putting down her tray. "Don't be hard on her. Ye men can get away with so much. One simple yes and we women bear all the burdens."

If Barrington's lips could press into a deeper line,

they'd fall from his solid chin. He ran a hand over his dark salted hair then shoved on his top hat. "Thank you for your time."

He dropped the coin onto the tray. It spun, making the air hiss. One, two, three rotations.

A swirling image came to Amora's memory, a vision of her friend's heart-shaped face, and her thin nose with deep amber eyes illuminated.

Amora caught the coin, and put it the barmaid's fingers. "This isn't my Sarah."

"I didn't think so. Let's go," he said.

The strength in his arms wrapped about her, shielding Amora as they retreated from the tavern. She needed his might to breathe, to shore up her spirit from this disappointment.

"Barrington, I'm so… I wish this hadn't wasted so much time."

"Nothing ventured, nothing gained. Besides, I was able to spend time with you without your mother or the vicar." His smile was warm, heating her numb insides. He buttressed her from the wind and lifted her over a patch of slushy snow.

With a hand on Barrington's shoulder, Amora climbed into his carriage. Her fingers dug into the heavy muscles hidden beneath the thick wool of his coat. Something instinctive, almost primal, made her imagine falling against him, burying herself in the strength of his chest, whispering, *Please fight my battles. Save me.*

But he couldn't.

No one else could. She had to be the one to save her sanity.

Turning, Amora looked through the window at the faded exterior of the public house. The answers she'd hoped to find weren't there. Maybe they didn't exist.

As the carriage lurched forward, Barrington reached over her head and closed the curtains, the gauzy fabric blurring the view of the wretched pub.

He cupped her hand within his, the large palm swallowing hers. For a moment, the chill in her limbs disappeared.

"We will find your Sarah." His tone sounded confident, but she could no longer share this optimism. What if Sarah had died, or worse? What if there was no Sarah at all, just a figment of her imagination lingering from captivity. Confidence eroding and sweat leaking out of her pores, she fanned her face.

"This was just our first try. I'll go back to the magistrate and learn more. Can you tell me some things about Sarah so I can be more certain of the person before I expose you to more disappointment?"

Barrington thought her weak, and she felt weak. Could one setback destroy her? She lifted her chin, feigning peace. "The barmaid had blond hair, like what I believe my Sarah has, but that wasn't her. My Sarah's eyes are amber."

"This is my fault. I should've done more checking before exposing you to the brazen miss." His hands spread as if he'd claim Amora's shoulders and sweep her into his arms, but he just touched the ceiling and sighed. "It's fine, my love. We'll find her yet."

Disappointment must be his ally. It was definitely hers.

"Look at you." He leaned close stroking her cheek, letting his fingers dance upon her lips. "This has upset you too much."

His touch lingered as if he'd kissed her. She pulled away and scampered to a far corner.

He held up his hands. "I didn't mean to. Actually, I *did*."

A small part of her wished he had tempted her. Her mind needed to be anywhere else, focused on something that could dissolve the pain, even for a moment.

He sank deeper into his seat and folded his arms. "I could have James take a longer route if you'd like. No sense rushing back to your mother. I wonder what decorating ideas are awaiting us. Perhaps new drapes, wall coverings in hues I can't see. Or maybe her Isis idols strewn in the parlor. Perhaps I should bring an ax, a Yahweh ax."

So typical of him, to assume a moment of despair brought on a full-fledged flight of despondency. She bristled and laced her fingers together. "I suppose a true victim of abduction needs a moment to gather her wits, otherwise I might find an attic or a bell tower."

He lifted his palms in the air again. His waistcoat swung wide exposing his grey shirt. James had removed all of Barrington's shiny buttons to observe full mourning of the King.

Funny how she missed the sound of his jingling brass. She was more sad at how everyone had to conform than at the King's passing.

He lowered his arms and tugged at his waistcoat. "I'm on your side, Amora. I don't know why someone would *lie*."

Gaping at his soft enunciation of the word, she couldn't let it go unchecked. She sat up straight and glared at him. "But you thought I did."

The sound of his shifting boots pierced the silence.

Her omission was a lie and once confirmed a liar to Barrington, always a liar. She'd never be anything more than a victim or a perjurer.

She siphoned a breath into her empty chest and refused to become upset at him for thinking so little of her. In two months, this part of her life would be over. He'd grant her a separation, and she'd go build a safe world back at Tomàs Manor. "It's fine, Barrington. I don't want to fight. We've got to make the most of this time to find the real Sarah."

The clip-clop of horse's hooves pounding along the streets vibrated the carriage. The shadows of a low sun encroached the window. Would they make it to Mayfair before it became dark? Maybe she could ask Barrington to light the lantern. "Barrington, could you—"

"Yes. Yes, I did think you lied."

His words sounded tight but small like a whisper, as if she'd forced him to admit the truth.

She rubbed her hands together, preparing for his frosty rebuke. "It's good to say things plain."

"Is that what you want me to do, brand you a liar, a person given to falsehoods? Does answering this plain way yield another black mark in your heart, the place where forgiveness doesn't live? At what point do I join the five-year forgiveness list like your mother? I must have something to look forward too."

She blinked at him unable to absorb the anger wetting his words. "I have no list."

"Yes, you do. Everyone does. We all make judgments as to who may enter their heart and who cannot." He dusted his knee as if a speck sat upon his onyx breeches. "It's best to know upon which list I hang."

If words could be naked, unclothed with polite sentiment, not carefully put together as a valet or lady's maid would do, then Barrington's had divested of everything, completely stripped bare in an emperor's parade of rawness.

"Isn't that right, Amora?"

Hardly able to breathe, she looked away from his twitching cheek, his smoldering eyes. Her fingers shook, not from fear, more so at the realization that she'd broken something inside him and didn't know how to fix him.

Maybe it wasn't possible to help another if one was broken too.

"What say you, Mrs. Norton? That is your title, though you are resigned to it."

Those eyes of hers felt raw as if they had a tear to offer, but she couldn't. A desert-like soul has no water. "I...I just wanted to be honest. I was wrong to have deceived you."

"Deceit? Which one, the abduction business or the keeping of me in sickness and in health as long as we both shall live?"

The cold air of the carriage swirled about her seeming to suck away her strength. Feeling small, as if the seat would swallow her, she looked down and shuffled her slippers. He'd changed his mind. He wasn't going to let her go. Forever imprisoned to his opinions, there was no room for Amora.

She tugged at her arms trying to hold on to her might, her will to be free, to know her own mind. Steadying herself she lifted her chin. "You agreed to a formal separation. Barrington Norton is a man of his word. Please do not take back my hope."

He pried off his top hat and fanned his head. "No."

Sending the brim sailing to his seat, he stretched out. "Remember what it means to me to make a promise?"

"I did keep my promise to you. I was faithful while you were at war."

"Can't you understand why I had doubts? I returned and you were so different, fretful of the dark, no painting or music - all masking your lack of trust, this insidious secret. Why Amora? How could you hide something so monstrous? Did you think I would blame you? How could I ever condemn you?"

"I, I tried—"

"Tried what? Tried to keep me from knowing your deepest pain. Did you think I was satisfied with only the pieces of you, you offered?" His voice lowered. "Five years, you walled off everything from me, but fear."

A groan left him. The temper that he'd kept locked away, surely growled for freedom. "Tell me, did you think of this monster every time I touched you in surprise? Was he in your thoughts whilst I slept at your side? Would he take my place when I arose early to work? The vicar said you talked of the monster when you miscarried. So he was there in my stead, presiding over our child's death."

Seething anger rippled over his face.

She wanted to close her eyes to his pain, the disappointments which were her fault, but her thoughts on the inside were worse. "I hoped marrying you, going on with life would take the memories away. Mama said you'd never marry me if you knew. I was desperate to try to live past this."

"Yes, the good pharaoh knows best. Her opinion weighed more than our pitiful love."

He sat back and started to chuckle. Could he have lost his wits too?

"My best friend jumped in front of me and took a

bullet meant to kill me, all because every private word we shared was of my coming home to you. How in love I was. How foolish of me. I don't think his sacrifice sufficient. Why return to a woman who neither trusted or loved me enough?"

"Barrington—"

"The doubts I had of our impulsive engagement were all well confirmed." He leaned forward. "Did you get some joy out of using my promise to free you from your mother and cousin? Now you are running back to the pharaoh."

Daggers diced up his words, slashing i's, impaling t's, all smoting her chest. The power he reserved for the Old Bailey's, he'd unleashed on her. She felt wounded and ashamed, never thinking she'd hurt him like this, never imagining she'd make his eyes cloud with agony, but she did. Patching together her warbling breath and hoping her voice held strong, she asked, "If my family betrayed me, why, why would you be different?"

His fist punched at his heart. "We are alike, misfits in this world. I wanted to fit your missing pieces. You were supposed to fill mine. Little did I know it was a losing trial, decided before the hearing. How much love could there have been in your heart if your opinion of me was so easily swayed?"

She opened her mouth then closed it. She felt herself slipping back into that place of defending her actions, of his opinions meaning more than hers. It was easy to do with Barrington exposing his honest heart. She forced her fingers to still and become like heavy stones in her lap, not rising to stroke his chin, not reaching for him to make his pain go away. "Rumors changed your thoughts. Cynthia whispered in your ear and you assumed I'd had an affair with Mr. Charleton."

"The year we became engaged was chaotic. My father died drunk in a brothel. Then my brother, the heir, was stricken with cholera just before his unit deployed. Grandfather signed me up to take his place before I could blink. In the middle of this turmoil, I fell hopelessly in love with a vibrant artist. For goodness sake, I can't even see half the things you painted."

His tone wasn't filled with regret. No, it was still white hot, searing her flesh, her conscience. "You're livid for loving me? I didn't force you to feel so much for me."

Barrington pumped one fist against the other. "I'm angry because you didn't love me enough. If you had, you would have told me all. You deprived me of being a better husband to you. In sickness and in health. Remember that vow? This omission has offered me a shell of the girl who once meant everything. I hate being cheated, even more than being told lies."

"Be a better husband? With all of your court duties? It bothered you to be on my schedule. I think you called it a leash to James."

"No, but I thought it." With a loud huff, he wiped at his face though sadness remained, twitching the cheek that announced the aches of a throbbing hip, or numbness at his grandfather's passing. "I'm not Mr. Tomas. I won't be ruled by a pharaoh, but at least your mother truly loved him. To be loved thoroughly and completely would make a man slay dragons, move mountains."

His tone slowed as the carriage turned onto their street. "But you couldn't love me that much."

Amora had nothing to say, nothing to make him feel better. Marriage didn't make her whole. It didn't take the monster away.

Yet, her insides were too busy dying a little more at how unfair this marriage had been to Barrington. She couldn't even give him a child to make it better for him.

He nodded, then picked up his hat twisting the brim within his palms. "When Miss Miller fed me rumors, I thought it was the truth. It nourished every doubt I had of us. If only I had known the truth. I could have been so much better, more considerate. I would have moved every mountain to keep your love."

"I did love you, Barr, but I can't remember what that feels like anymore. Love can't be this constant stew of hurt."

"I'm not looking for some grand declaration, but don't make all of our problems my fault. If we have any chance of…" He rammed backwards and slid his top hat over his eyes. "We won't be effective at piecing together this mystery, if you can't tell me everything. It definitely won't work if I am continually punished for my own wrongheaded conclusions and you find no fault with your own."

The carriage stopped. He popped up, opened the door, and helped her down. "Go inside."

"You're not retiring?"

"I'm heading to the Lincoln's Inn. It's barely seven. I will be back at Mayfair before 10:30. I am a man of my word. Know that at least."

He leaned against the carriage, and stayed there until she made it up the steps and across the threshold. She dashed to the window in time to see him join James atop their carriage and take the reins.

Barrington had never told her anything like that, about feeling unequally yoked. Hadn't she shown him love? She'd fretted over him, and constantly wanted him near. Didn't that count for something?

She put a hand to her mouth, those truthful fingers trembling. Maybe it didn't. She'd accepted his proposal all those years ago because she did love him, but the years apart were hard. Then her abduction changed everything. Over these last five years of marriage, had she reached for him out of fear or love?

Her heart sank low as she remembered craving his presence, needing his strong arms to snuggle her against him, to prove the nightmares weren't real, that she wasn't still trapped in a dank cell. Fear had been the driving force of everything, not love.

Barrington was a smart man. He knew the difference.

Chapter Eight: An Honest Drive

Two months to woo a wife, find a missing person, and capture a killer was an incredibly short period of time. No days should be squandered brooding, but that is exactly what Barrington did. He took two weeks to sulk over making a fool of himself to Amora in their outing to Whitby's. A man shouldn't admit but to three feelings: hunger, sleep or lust. This touchy feely stuff about love and not enough love, that should be left to poets.

Barrington was no poet, just a barrister who'd won his first case since his return to London, one with mounds of paper and books stacked to the ceiling, covering his desk at the Lincoln's Inn.

Beakes found an obscure coroner's notes about a young woman's partially nude body found on the side of the road. She'd been strangled, the date matching Smith's description, June 11, 1813.

It still didn't prove Smith had been in league with the infamous Dark Walk Abductor, but he had worked for a murderer. Someone that potentially had the means and influence to arrange Smith's being apprehended with the coining evidence.

Shoving his papers an inch, Barrington wanted to flop upon the expanse of his desk. He had a bigger case to solve, or come to terms with. Reading through the accounts of the Dark Walk Abductor's true victims sounded a lot more like Amora's story. Could her monster be the Dark Walk Abductor?

If this was true, she suffered more cruelly than he could ever have imagined. Chains, beatings, abuse. He shook the filth from his thoughts and headed out of his office to his awaiting vehicle. This would be an early day. He couldn't bear to read another statement of misery and not punch through a wall.

Listless, he trudged up the cobblestone path to Mayfair's door just shy of sunset. Amora should be pleased. Though his thoughts of winning her back pretty much died with his outburst, he still needed to make sure she didn't become anxious. It was immaterial that she didn't suffer as he did from this oppressive feeling of longing.

He couldn't stop thinking of her, remembering the turn of her countenance when she didn't correct him, nor the sound of her tossing in her bed from his adjoining chamber.

Annoyed with himself, he dragged across Mayfair's threshold and offered the smiling Mrs. Gretling his hat, coat, and gloves. "What have Mrs. Tomàs and Mrs. Norton done today? Picked new curtains, burned the Norton furnishings? Set up a temple in the mews."

The housekeeper set his articles down on the show table. "Not much today, but a great many vendors arrived measuring things." She eyed him and pointed to his head. "Sir, you—"

A wave of laughter came from the parlor. A child's giggles?

Since when did his town home have children? Plodding toward the noise, a little girl rammed into him with a dripping paintbrush in her hand.

An indeterminate color splashed his breeches.

She fingered her spiraling curls as her lips slumped into a frown. "Sorry, sir."

His angry heart melted a little at the penitent look the child offered. The vicar's daughter would steal hearts one day. Hopefully, she'd know what to do with them once she had them. He took out a handkerchief and mopped at the stain. "Is there a master work of art associated with that brush, Miss Rebecca?"

The cherub smiled and tugged him into the room. "Mr. Norton, come see what Mrs. Norton taught me."

He let the gleeful girl lead him to the sofa where Amora sat. A light colored gown nestled her limbs, sculpting her long neck. In her arms snuggled a babe. She looked calm and natural. A pain stabbed at his gut and stretched to his unloved heart. If only their child had lived, that would've given her joy. Amora needed more joy.

With the lift of her chin, she offered a smile. "It's not dark yet and you're at Mayfair." Her eyes widened as the babe cooed. "Yes, look at the man in the horsey wig."

He touched at his hair and felt the stiff tufted curls of his court headpiece. Reaching up, he pulled off the thing and stashed it in his tailcoat. "I've been wearing it since the morning session at the Old Bailey."

"Are you rushing for a reason, Barrington?" Amora's eyes stretched wide, proud almond shaped wonders gleaming. "Has the magistrate offered more Sarahs?"

"Not yet." He hadn't bothered the man since the last disastrous outing. Barrington needed more from Amora, more about the abduction. There had to be a clue in the way she was taken that would separate her circumstances from all the Dark Walk Abductor's victims. Lord, he needed there to be two villains, not one. He shook his head. What a prayer to pray?

Shuddering again on the inside from mentally putting Amora's abduction together with those heinous crimes, he forced himself to survey the room. There was nothing new, just an easel behind the sofa. Mrs. Tomas's Isis idols stood watch on the mantel. Perhaps, he needed to set a Bible beside it or get Wilson to bring over a cross or that Yahweh ax, so he could chop down the pagan to bits.

Alas, that wouldn't do well for the truce. His mother-in-law hadn't been so prickly. Let the pharaoh build her pyramids or drapery. He hadn't exactly been a model for Christianity, jumping to accusations and condemning his own wife. No, he needed to live more of his faith to sway anyone.

The little girl's tugs led him to the easel. Risking getting more paint on his clothes, he picked up the canvas and released the perfunctory oohs and aahs. "Ah, Miss Rebecca your art is lovely.

He squinted and stretched his eyes. "What type of fruit is in the bowl?" Setting it down, he fiddled with his glasses, as if that would provide clarity.

"They're limes. Mrs. Norton made me work on shading. Limes in a clover green bowl on an emerald-colored tablecloth."

Green upon green, upon green. Yes. Amora hated him. He rubbed his brow. "Everything looks the same as yesterday, neat room, pretty wife, and handsome mother-in-law." He plodded to the fireplace and tapped a garniture vase next to the others, centering it in spite of the fourteen-inch high wooden god. "Almost perfect."

Amora burped the baby then handed him to her mother. "Then to what do we owe the pleasure of this change in your schedule?"

He leaned against the mantle and folded his arms. "Time is wasting. I need more information to make progress on our project."

"I'm a project?"

Mrs. Tomàs pattered over to him. The babe fisted his hand onto her mobcap. He grabbed it and exposed her ash-black hair. "Surely, Mr. Norton, you and Amora can let this abduction business be done with. It's over for us."

He took the struggling boy from her arms, swaddling the lively thing in his creamy pinafore. Such a strong, healthy child. "It's not over until someone pays for the crime."

The little boy settled and grabbed his nose.

If he allowed his heart to be jealous, it would be greener than whatever Rebecca painted on the canvas. Amora played family with the vicar's children. Dying a little more on the inside from his own withered dreams of family, of a happy home with the woman he loved, Barrington forced his tone to be sweet. "My wife knows I must learn all the facts. It's just my way."

He bounced the boy again, enjoying the tiny eager eyes of the little fellow. "And where is the good vicar to complete our group?"

Amora's lips pouted. She hadn't glared at him directly since the argument, but now violet lights beamed at him. "You know how to hold a baby very well. I should've known you'd take to it easily."

She clasped her hands in her lap and looked down. "The vicar should be here soon."

Blasted man and his adorable children making them feel the loss of their child again. Blasted heart for hurting so much. *Get a handle on your emotions, Norton.* "Sweetheart, I'll need to ask you questions. Starting with what you do remember is the best way to make progress. We can work in my study or go for a drive."

The slam of the front door and the cackling laughter of Mrs. Gretling announced the vicar's irritating arrival.

Amora's gaze lifted, her countenance seemed to smooth. What a great confidant he must be for her.

"There's the vicar. Coming to retrieve his dear children. They must all stay for dinner. Mama has been helping Mrs. Gretling."

Barrington continued to make faces at the little boy to hide his covetousness or convey his sympathy to poor Mrs. Gretling having to endure the pharaoh directly.

The vicar waltzed through the door and headed straight for Barrington. "Thank you, Mr. Norton."

Almost wishing for another moment, Barrington handed him the boy.

The vicar lifted his son into the air and twirled him.

Rebecca came running and gripped the man's leg. "Papa, come see what I've done."

"Yes, moppet, I've thought of nothing else but coming here to see the wonderful things Mrs. Tomàs and Mrs. Norton have taught you."

He wandered behind the sofa to his child's painting, his steps, so happy, so complete.

Barrington's jealous heart stewed again, but he stepped to his wife. "Well, Amora, a drive or my office? Let's get on with these questions."

The vicar looked over his shoulder. "I think it's a wonderful idea for you and Mr. Norton to go for a drive. That will give Mrs. Tomàs and me plenty of time to discuss our next big outing."

Mrs. Tomàs joined the vicar, standing at his side. "Yes, Amora, go put on your walking dress. It's still full-mourning outside these walls. The air will do you good. She felt a bit poorly this morning, Mr. Norton."

Amora stood, her motion slow, like she'd become dizzy.

"Are you up to this, madam wife? We can postpone."

She shrugged. "I'll go put on something appropriate." She looked again toward the vicar, then headed out of the room.

Wilson gave his son to Mrs. Tomàs. "Becky, go with this dear lady and get cleaned up for dinner."

With nods and another hug, the vicar's children left the parlor with Mrs. Tomàs, leaving only the men.

Wilson traipsed toward Barrington. "Mrs. Norton told me of the disastrous meeting with Sarah Jenkins."

Puffing up his chest, Barrington steeled himself for the admonishment. "Go ahead and tell me how wrongheaded this is."

"On the contrary, Mr. Norton, keep helping. I've tried to get her to talk about her captivity to get the fear stuck out of her head, but she becomes reticent in the middle. With you, she might be braver."

"So she won't tell you?" Barrington almost felt a portion of glee at having any advantage with Amora. "Wilson, what do you think I should do?"

The vicar yanked on his waistcoat and stalked about, proud like a peacock. He went to the window and tugged on the curtain. "Keep her out until it's dark. Make her confront the fear."

"Take her to the park or somewhere in nature to distract her?"

"I'm not as familiar with London as you, but somewhere she can let her guard down. Be gentle, but don't stop until you get the whole story of her abduction. Reassure her that it wasn't her fault. If she can talk about it, she might be able to overcome the terror she carries. No matter how reasonable she seems, it's still with her. It lives in each breath."

Wilson pivoted, his face absent of cheer, lips etched in the deepest frown. "Don't let her become too fearful. Mr. Playfair's and my cousin, Harriet Westbrook Shelley, grew despondent and drowned herself in one of those parks. I assume that means all the London parks aren't filled with flowers and music."

Barrington winced, remembering poor Harriet's story. Her suicide was in the papers with all the torrid details of her abandonment and secret pregnancy. Women suffered greatly under scandal. His stubborn heart softened again for Amora and the choices she made.

Draped in a dark gown with black velvet edging the hem and a crisp straw bonnet, she stood at the door. Amora bit her lip then leveled her shoulders. "I'm ready."

Barrington nodded. "Have a good dinner, Vicar. Come along, my dear."

He scooped up his greatcoat and received her arm. Barrington didn't appreciate a lecture from another man about his wife, but the warning felt true. If he couldn't find a way to solve this crime, there would be another low moment, and it would challenge her resolve to live. Right now, he didn't think this side of glory would win.

* * *

Amora tapped the carriage seat, her short nails clicking upon a tufted button as she counted the seconds between horse clomps. How could they be stuck in heavy traffic? James, Barrington's man-of-all-work, was very capable. For their last outing to Whitby, the fellow had whisked them through London as if they flew upon sparrow's wings.

The sun lowered in the horizon. Her chest shuddered. Evening was approaching. Did Barrington intend for them to go down every busy road, wasting time?

At this pace, they wouldn't return to Mayfair before dark. Was that what he wanted?

A seed of terror stuck in her head and rooted. The last time she rode that way was the night she miscarried. Her temples began to pound. Amora struggled to lift her chin.

Barrington sat silent in the seat opposite her, staring in her direction. What was he thinking? Where did he instruct James to go? Until today, her husband seemed distant. Physically, he'd lived at Mayfair, offered polite comments, came in and out of the town house like clockwork, but one look into his grey eyes announced the truth. There was nothing there, as if he were hundreds of miles away.

Yet, something had changed when he held Jackson. Barrington's lenses possessed a spark, so warm and volatile, it shot heat across the room. The vicar's young son grew sleepy, at peace within Barrington's arms. Being in his arms always made her feel better, too.

When the carriage turned onto Park Lane, her spirit sank deeper. They headed to Hyde Park, that pretentious place. Maybe Barrington wanted people to see them together to squelch the rumors of an upset in the Norton household. How much talk did the partygoers unleash after the fight with Mr. Charleton at the Dowager's ball?

Barrington blew into his gloved hands. "Why are you frowning? Can't a husband take his wife for a ride through the park? You love nature. I remember that."

She shrank back from the window, tugging her palms into her lap. "The whole surface of Hyde Park is dry crumbling sand, not a vestige or hint of grass. You did not get me out of Mayfair for a nature walk."

"You are right. I thought we'd watch the sun set while you tell me what happened the day you were abducted."

Her heart pulsed. The fingers she wanted stilled trembled against her knee. She counted in silence until she couldn't keep her peace. "Take me home."

"Amora, we need to talk away from distractions." His voice sounded sad and held an awful note of pity. "If you're not able, I don't know how--"

Fourteen, fifteen. "Don't." She lifted her face and stopped numbering nail heads in the floorboards. "Don't use that tone, ever. I can't stand it."

"Then tell me what happened. How did he take you? I have to know."

"Why? So you can tell me how my stubbornness betrayed me? How daft I was being out alone? I do that daily."

"Amora, I've prosecuted a few abduction cases. It shouldn't be the woman's fault if she's tricked or taken by force. I know with no doubt that you didn't agree."

"That's not how the law goes. Papa and I came to some of your early trials before your enlistment. Any consent is consent."

"You came to one?" A smile over took his lips. That spark made his grey eyes bloom again. "I know you didn't agree. Tell me what happened." He leaned over and calmed her fingers. "Tell me how the man stole your joy."

She knocked away his hands and folded her arms. "What do you mean?"

"You don't smile, not very often. I thought it was me who took it, but I believe whatever you lived through claimed it. Your joy and your smile are in your abductor's pocket. Trust me enough to tell me what happened that day. Nothing will hurt again. I'm here for you now."

The monster couldn't have any more of her. None. But neither could Barrington.

The carriage stopped. Without another thought, she pressed on the door and trudged outside. Luckily, they weren't near the Tour, the part of the large park where the fashionable needed to be seen. She didn't want to be seen. No one should judge her anymore.

She crossed a pebbled stretch then stopped, looking into the murky waters of the Serpentine. The setting sun made the surface a swirl of red and orange.

"The water has thawed." Barrington plodded close, scooped up a stone and skipped it across the surface. The rock bounced four times, then sank deep below. "It's very cold, but after a few minutes, you won't care. Harriet Westbrook drowned here. She killed her unborn child too."

A shudder ran up Amora's spine. The fight to stay above the waters of Clanville came to her mind. Her skin pimpled.

An arm came about her shoulder. She turned and gripped it hard, clutching it as if it were the branch that kept her from falling immediately into the Clanville

River.

"You won't do it. I've got you. It's good you're done playing with water."

Amora shook free. "I didn't jump off that cliff to punish you."

"I know. You are a strong woman, Amora. A clod like me can't make you so desperate that dying seems better. Tell me why you didn't stay on that portico."

She couldn't look at him. Couldn't say aloud the weakness she'd almost surrendered to.

"Amora, however the monster took you, you did nothing to deserve it. Tell me what happened. I need the clues to find Sarah."

Hot tears slipped her lashes. "I don't remember much. I'd argued with Mama, grabbed my paints, and slipped from the house."

"What was the time of day?"

She pressed her temples. "Late in the evening, a couple of hours before sunset."

He nodded, his chin bussing her bonnet. "What did you paint?"

Pictures of trees cluttered her head, spinning images of green and brown. Her pulse thundered. She felt light-headed, weak.

Maybe Barrington caught her or maybe she turned and fell into him, but she was in his arms, safe and warm against his greatcoat.

"That time is over. We're just gathering the facts."

"It's not over for me. I'm still there in that cellar every night. Sometimes Sarah's there. Sometimes not, but I hear the others."

"What others?"

"I wasn't the first or the last person my abductor took.

There were more. I heard them all screaming for help, and I could do nothing but wait my turn." Her throat clogged with sobs and violent shakes seized her body. "They still cry out at me, but I couldn't give in to the monster to stop him. I couldn't help them. I couldn't."

Barrington brought her head deeper into his chest. Very slowly, he tightened his arms about her. "A madman's wrath, it's not your fault. Oh God, help her to know it's not her fault."

Amora pushed back from his safety. "But it is!" Her voice warbled, everything seemed wobbly but she had to confess. "He...he made me his pet and said he'd stop hurting the girls if I would be his. I couldn't do it. I had promised you to stay yours and only yours."

He put a hand to her neck, stroking the strain in the muscles. "You can't control the monster. I've seen this type of evil in the courts. That hate-filled hunger won't be quenched. It must be stopped."

"My abductor hurt them all, even Sarah. My fault."

She pushed free, refusing to look into Barrington's eyes. Where was the carriage? Where. Blinded by tears, she trudged forward. She'd beg James to take her back to Mayfair.

A strong arm grabbed her about her middle and spun her around. She struggled but couldn't fight his strength. The rich smell of bergamot on Barrington's skin calmed her. She stilled and let Barrington hold her.

"Your dense vicar said you were haunted by the terror of the villain, but that can't be. You're the bravest woman I know."

That was a lie. Palms flat, she beat against his chest. The iron wouldn't give. It became stronger. He drew her off her feet, burying her against his starched cravat, beneath the layers of his tailcoat's smooth wool. His bergamot scent became stronger kissing her nose. The memories of awaking in Barrington's arms, safe and warm overwhelmed her. Tired, so tired of fighting, she slumped against him.

"It's guilt that keeps you in bondage. Guilt over the girls you couldn't save. Guilt because you are alive, when Miss Druby, Gerald Miller's poor girl, isn't."

"I am guilty and no one can end my sentence." She tugged free again and took a few steps toward the pond.

"I live that guilt, Amora. Every time I shave my chin, I know my friend Miller isn't. I have dreams. I see him, the man who loved me like a brother, jumping into the bullet's path. I witness the blood, the withering of his face."

Gerald Miller and Barrington were very close. Miller followed him into the service. "At least he died honorably, not consumed by a villain."

"No, Amora, but he was brave like you."

"I'm not that brave or I'd jump in that pond and make all the hurting go away. I just don't know if the hereafter is any better. Maybe it's constant torment. Maybe Isis is waiting in a garden for me."

He grabbed her arms and swung her around, away from the pond. "God, the true God would not be pleased. Neither would I."

"The same One that took Papa? The One that killed our babe?" She cocked her head to the side to watch the emotions sweeping across his face. "The One that doomed us?"

His lip twitched. A tremble set in his cheek.

"He's not pleased with me, Barrington. How much worse could it get?"

"I'm not a theologian. I'm a barrister. Taking your life is the easy way out. It takes guts to live. It takes a stomach of iron to uncover the identity of the monster. Together, we can locate him and set the sword of the law upon his head."

"How is one to do that? How?"

"If we can get the fiend to justice or at least blacken his name, it will lift up all his victims. It will make Sarah, wherever she is, a truth-teller. Miss Druby's parents will have a villain's identity to soothe their pain. That's how we help them, and we can do it together."

She squinted at Barrington. The setting sun shrouded his silhouette as if he wore gleaming armor.

"Let's return to the carriage."

They walked back in silence. When they arrived at the carriage, Barrington put his hands onto her hips, and with firm fingers, hoisted her inside. "I have a lantern so we can stay for a while even in the dark. Or I'll take you back now, if this is too much."

Not sure she could face her mother or the vicar with her thoughts jumbled, she nodded her consent. Yet, as the world dimmed outside, her breath caught. Other patches of air wouldn't come down. She hit at her chest to make her lungs work. "Hurry with the light."

He caught her hands. "One, two, three like a waltz, sniff some air. One, two, three. Like when we dance."

She peered out the window and counted twinkling jewels, a night's sky of stars blinking to his rhythm. Pulse slowing, she slipped free from his too comforting hands and leaned back along the bench.

"I found you one evening about to fall asleep on the floor. Is it better there?"

The hoot of a distant owl, a cricket's chirping seeped

through the walls. Weren't those the noises that had comforted her in the dark root cellar? She pulled her knees onto the seat and laid her head upon them. The music of the creatures lulled her. "I don't know, but Sarah would hum just like you."

"This woman possessed a deep masculine voice?"

"No."

He struck the lamp and the light glowed in the dark compartment. "Continue."

"We'd sleep on the ground back to back, in a feeble attempt to protect ourselves. You could hear the monster's breathing, his watching us."

A rush of heat surrounded her, turning her stomach. She pushed at her straw bonnet, allowing her forehead to cool. "If I get sick on you, know that I don't mean to."

"Couldn't be much worse than when you threw dinner at me." A chortle rumbled in his chest as he loosened his neck cloth. "The night is not so bad. Remember the nightingale? It sang for us in the moonlight. Goodness, I love balconies. It reminds me of the first time I kissed you."

She closed her eyes for a moment and pictured Barrington on that balcony. His voice mirrored that time, filled with peaks and valleys, maybe a little nervousness.

He cleared his throat. "Your nightingale. It's my favorite of all your works. I kept it and the one you made from ash."

Stomach twisting, she watched the lantern. Hints of blue and orange swirled about the charred wick. Was he intentionally keeping the flame low?"

"Be at ease, dear girl." Barrington began to hum again. His voice was deep and sweet to her ears. The rhythm, the cadence, it was the same beat with which he helped her to gain air.

"What is that tune?"

"Something I heard the last time we went to St. Georges. It's a hymn about grace, about being blind and now seeing. I so wish I hadn't been so blind. I could've been so much more understanding. I would've found ways to grow your love."

She moved her palms against the rough leather of the seat. "I feel like I am losing my wits. Do you think that is what King George or Harriet felt like before succumbing?"

"I know not about them, but you are as sane as anyone. Your struggle is just a bit harder. We have to trust that you will choose to fight every day for wellness, to choose to smile. Hopefully, God will use your dunderhead of a husband to make your burdens easier. That's my new prayer."

There he was, being noble about their ruined marriage. If she were a stronger person, she wouldn't have turned herself into an unlovable rag doll. "God has to be blind, Barrington. Why did He leave me captive for almost two months? Why didn't He save the girls? And why can't He heal my mind so I can forget?"

"I don't know. Some of the trials I've prosecuted made me doubt God's grace. There is evil in this world with no other mission than to kill, steal, and destroy. Then I look at the innocence of a child like Jackson or Rebecca, full of wonder and curiosity, perfect in so many ways. There is a God, for He made them. We have to fight the despair, the questions with no answers. I am going to trust that He will turn our sorrow to joy. That He will give us the strength to see the beauty in ashes, just like your nightingale.

Barrington's fingers sought hers. "I have a few more questions, but I'll make them brief. Answer what you can."

He took a deep breath and took off his spectacles. "Did he strike you?"

"Yes."

His boot started tapping the floor. "Did he bind you?"

"Yes. He chained us."

Barrington's foot became very still. He leaned closer and mouthed, "Did he abuse you? Force himself upon you?"

Images twisted in her mind. A memory of a blow to her cheek obscured everything. "I don't know. I can't remember."

He sat back and returned his lenses to their proper place. "Did he abuse others?"

"Yes, then he got rid of them. Please, enough. Don't make me say anymore, not tonight."

He leaned forward and grasped her hand, stilling her fidgeting. "I'm going to find this man. He will face justice."

One look in his smoldering silver eyes, the pride in his straight back, his wonderful swarthy skin and she knew he meant what he said. He would at last be her champion if she let him, but this battle wasn't his. "Can we go back to Mayfair?"

"You've given me enough for now." He joined her on her seat and tapped on the roof. Soon the carriage lurched forward. "I'm not as knowledgeable about God as your vicar friend, but I know God would never send a man to chain you."

He took off his gloves and put his warm palm on her cheek. "God wouldn't order a fiend to abuse his handiwork. You and the other girls didn't deserve this."

She let Barrington's words soak in, but it didn't feel true. God knew who was responsible, but He let the man go free. How many others were taken or killed like Nan Druby?

Barrington's arm slipped behind her. "Here's a shoulder to snuggle against, in a purely non-husbandly way of course."

If she'd had the energy to chuckle, she would have, but Amora felt drained, deflated. Instead, she drew against him.

The quiet cabin, the small light of the lantern, this might be romantic if she weren't dark on the inside.

The carriage kept a slow pace along the streets. Barrington sat frozen. He didn't try to embrace her or kiss her. Yet, this closeness was so much better. He was a strong tower, and she could choose to run deeper into his arms or sit as she was on the outskirts of his affection, venturing only as much of her heart as she felt safe to offer.

When she opened her eyes, the carriage had stopped at Mayfair.

He climbed down and lifted his arms to her. "See? The dark isn't so bad."

She clasped his fingers and climbed down. "Vicar Wilson said the other women he counseled were afraid of the dark, too."

The muscles in his forearm tensed. "How many others has the good vicar seen?"

"I don't know, but I'm sure they weren't angry at God for stealing their father."

She bit her lip, and then dashed ahead of him into the bright lights at the entry of Mayfair. Focusing on the sconces, she filled her lungs. Barrington could never understand how she ran from Tomàs Manor filled with stubborn hatred at her father's passing. Papa was everything. The evening of her abduction, she had slapped her brushes against the canvas with anger and tears, all while screaming at God. Yes, God smote her then and He'd keep doing it. What would be the next punishment?

Chapter Nine: The Best Plans

The sixth week of his fabulous plan to woo his wife into reconsidering a permanent separation felt as successful as the other five, another utter failure. Barrington was desperate, pouring through old complaints and witness statements of abduction victims during the day and trying to appear relaxed and amiable at night. It was harder than he could imagine balancing court and his new obsession with finding his wife's abductor.

Even harder realizing he couldn't help Amora.

His wife barely came out of her bedchamber. When she did, she seemed sickly. Her stomach, probably nervous tension had her vomiting in the mornings, and slow and sluggish the rest of the day. Though she said she'd be fine to attend his mentor's ball tonight, she groused at Barrington when he suggested having a doctor see her. With everything that had happened to her, he understood and wouldn't press her.

"Sir, what do you think?" The jeweler held the simple pair of diamond earrings up to the store window. The shine of the white crystals blinded with the noon sun. Barrington had never seen more perfect gems.

Amora would adore them, that is if he gave them to her. Their anniversary was several months away, but he'd tried just about everything else to sway her. Would she be open to bribes?

He'd pay for an extension of his two-month deadline. She was well worth the effort.

"The clarity will make yer lady swoon." The man put the elongated ovals into a tiny felt box. "The wife or the mistress will be appreciative. I am too. Business has been a little slow. Can't wait for the world to go to half-mourning to allow for extravagance again."

"They are for my wife." What was wrong with London? Did a man have to have a mistress to purchase jewelry? He could understand Amora questioning his fidelity after arriving on several occasions to Mayfair smelling of Cynthia's chrysanthemums. But a shopkeeper questioning his vows? Barrington shook his head. "You know where to send the bill."

He stuffed the box into his pocket and left the shopkeeper. Winding down Sackville Street, he crossed another. His steps thudded, matching the ticking of the clock in his study. The one he'd checked his pulse against after reading his mentor's notes on the Dark Walk Abductor. Hessing had tried to mount a case a few years back, but couldn't find the culprit.

In these victims' accounts, there were no Sarahs, but there was a Mary and an Elizabeth. Their interviews of being dragged away, of being locked in a dark cell and chained matched Amora's. Could the man who took Amora also be the Dark Walk Abductor? And if so, how to prove it?

His heart cringed at the thought of Amora taking the witness box at the Old Bailey. No, it had to be two separate villains. Clanville and London were hours apart. Yet, his instincts made his rib, his internal truth detector vibrate, his mind settled more and more upon the notion of one monster.

It would explain why no one in London found the girls. Was the monster hiding his depravity in a remote place between the small country village and the big city? That could be how he escaped justice.

The noises of merchants and rushing carriages pressed every side. The perfumery of musk scents clouded the sidewalk. He picked up his pace, before any lilac, Amora's lilac, found his nose. His heart couldn't take it.

She'd be leaving him for good in a fortnight if he didn't come up with a miracle. Maybe God would give him a reprieve when he met with the magistrate. He knew more, so maybe he'd find a new clue to Sarah's identity. This time he'd ask for the deaths attributed to the Dark Walk Abductor.

Shoving a hand into his onyx coat, he gripped the small box. Maybe he wouldn't make a big fuss of an early anniversary present and just give the earrings to her to wear for Hessing's party tonight.

Gong. A church bell sounded above.

Blinking, Barrington examined his perch. He stood upon the steps of the grand portico of St. Georges. He put his hand on one of the cold stone columns supporting the overhang. Somehow, he'd walked all the way to the church.

Maybe the vicar, his wife's chummy friend, could tell him about the other victim's he'd counseled. Something wasn't quite right about the man, but that could be Barrington's jealousy talking.

He slipped into the church and tossed a few pence into the bucket then hopped into a boxed pew. The church was quiet. Magical light streamed through the colored panes highlighting the painting of the Last Supper.

How ironic, the light, which Amora craved, highlighted the table on the canvas. Was that a sign not to give up?

Blast it. His eyes widened as he tamped down his impatient thoughts in the holy place.

Blowing out steam, he shook his head. He was a man of action. What could he do? If he tried again to convince her to stay, would she be angry?

Was there anything else he could lose?

He took off his hat and dipped his chin. "Lord, You made me a warrior in the battlefield and in the courts. How do I fight for my wife? I thank You for the double portion of patience You've given me, but please add just a smidgen of hope."

A tap on his shoulder summoned him from his worship. He leaned back upon the pew.

Wilson towered above. "Mr. Norton. Is something wrong?"

"Well, you should know. You've been in our lives quite a while. Yet, I know very little about you."

"Would you like to see my seminary scores? I can save you the trouble. They were abysmal." The light charcoal colored pants and cut of his dark jacket made the man seem quite pulled together, if not for the rumpled waistcoat and windblown hair. "What is it you truly wish to know?"

Barrington straightened his posture and tugged on his

top hat. "Tell me about the other women you counseled?"

Wilson smiled. "Can you be more specific? Seems a widowed vicar gets a great deal of offers for dinner and ministry-making."

"That's not an answer, vicar. I want to know if you counseled any of the Dark Walk Abductor's victims."

He stood erect. "Yes, I have. If you count Mrs. Norton, that would be five in all."

Barrington's ears stopped working. He must be staring at the man witless. "Please repeat what you said."

"Yes, Mr. Norton. Her story is so similar, too similar. I highly doubt two men could operate in the same manner."

Blinking, to make his brainbox work, he stepped closer to the vicar. "Why didn't you say this before?"

"Let's talk later. Mrs. Hessing is in my office. She just stopped in to invite me to her party. She says you and her husband are colleagues."

"Yes." It was all Barrington could muster and breathe at the same time, thinking of his mentor's wife and her ready ear for gossip.

James bounded down the aisle. "Here you are, sir. You told me to keep you on task for your appointment."

The meeting with the magistrate. He nodded at his trusted servant. "Wilson, this is my Man-of-all-work, James. We shall talk. I have to know all."

"Go to your appointment, Mr. Norton. I haven't any good answers. One lady is committed, another disappeared, two had very short lives. When I heard your wife's fevered words, that's when I knew. That's why I warned you. So far, you've kept her safe."

The implicit warning of how long, how long would

Amora be safe and well, hung in the air and for that Barrington had no answers.

Frowning, the minister turned and plodded out of the sanctuary. "See you tonight."

James reached into his mantle and retrieved a note. "Mr. Beakes sent this for you."

Barrington pounded near and took it. Beakes's scrawl indicated he wanted to meet today, but with the magistrate's meeting there wasn't time.

The magistrate's meeting was more important. He had to find Amora's Sarah. *Please, Lord, I need to find this woman, just to prove Amora's not a Dark Walk Abductor's victim.*

Beakes's note burned in his hands. He wouldn't want to meet unless he'd acquired a new client for Barrington or made progress locating the person impersonating Gerald Miller.

Barrington crushed the paper. This was a distraction away from solving his wife's problems. He slid the note into his pocket. He'd meet with Beakes tomorrow. Amora's interest came first even before his lost friend, Gerald.

James straightened his tricorn as he opened the church door. "May I see the jewels, sir?"

Barrington waited until he'd climbed into his carriage before retrieving the gift from his coat. The hinge of the case whined as he showed the earrings.

"You have the best taste, Mr. Norton. Such long ovals. Length begets loving."

A deep sigh fled Barrington's lips as he closed the box. "No, James. The saying is length begets loathing."

A twinkle set in the man's wizen eyes. "So it does, Mr. Norton. So it does. But may I offer advice?"

"You usually do." Couldn't stop the man if he tried.

James tapped his boot on the bottom of the wheel knocking a spoke. "The missus might not be as impressed with your expression of loving."

Barrington furrowed his brow. "The gems are the best. I want the best for my wife, James. I've got nothing left to offer her."

"You're a good employer, a very excellent man, but you don't understand being told *no*." James thumbed his livery at his chest. "I live no. My Ester's death was a no. And when England impressed our oldest..." His voice broke, then returned to his even, deep tone. "Took him for her Navy, I had to let them and pray for the best, but I'm used to *no*. Accept this one, sir, and pray for your next steps."

Barrington lifted his gaze to his manservant. "I didn't know. Maybe I could do something."

His dark brown eyes widened then slimmed as his head lowered. "Your hands are mighty full. I've made peace with it. Now, let's get you to your meeting."

"Yes. Take me to magistrate."

The door closed, shadowing Barrington within the carriage. No time for his wife or his faithful advocate, he had so many chits to right. He took out pages from his war Bible and thumbed the leaves. How would Barrington get along if the answer to saving his marriage was *no*?

Chapter Ten: Mooning and Mourning at a Ball

With Mama on one arm and Amora on the other, her husband escorted them into Wadling Hall, Hessing's brilliant estate. Not as gilded as the dowager's, but the house glistened with marbled stairs and beautiful lights everywhere.

Amora adorned her obsidian mourning cape. Scarlet velvet ribbon zig-zagged the dark hem, swishing from side to side as they took the steps. The gown was another gift from Mother. She'd went into town and had a dressmaker fashion something stylish and divine in the sea of black and grey mourning garbs. Amora enjoyed the kindness. Mama was on her side. Well, at least for now.

She looked back at the woman and smiled, hoping she felt Amora's gratitude. Or maybe she, like Barrington, could surmise the wall still in place about her heart.

Sighing, she glanced at Barrington as a myriad of servants in crimson and white descended, separating them, taking his top hat and the ladies' heavier capes.

Barrington led them forward. Other than assisting Amora into the carriage and asking if she felt up to attending, he hadn't said much. He didn't try to keep her hand. No easy quips left his lips. No, they were too busy forming a frown.

"Barrington, is all well?"

Handsome as he was in the crisp black and white formal wear, his mind appeared to be elsewhere. He fumbled with his pocket watch. "Yes. Let's say hello to Mrs. Hessing."

Why did his odd manner send waves of concern to her roiling middle?

She steadied herself. The morning's nausea had returned. Her stomach hadn't been this unpredictable since...

No, she couldn't be pregnant.

That would be the height of irony. That one time of being intimate with Barrington four months ago, before everything went crazy. Before she let her mind go crazy. She blinked her eyes and tamped down this new crazed thought.

Barrington leaned close to her ear. "Are you suffering? Should I take you home?"

No more than usual. "I'm well. This night is to set your career back on the right path."

He sighed and led her forward. "Yes, part of our two-month agreement. Since I haven't changed your mind or made good on my other promises, you don't have to do anything but enjoy yourself tonight."

"I can do more, Barr. I want to do more."

His gaze tangled with hers, then he looked away. "Come along, Mrs. Norton."

It was good he started moving. She couldn't say yes to

the heat in his stare.

In front of them sat a marble staircase. A glistening chandelier hung in the middle. It appeared to sway to the musician's tempo.

They joined the line to be greeted by Mrs. Hessing. Their hostess's onyx gown looked so beautiful with heavy lace on each cap sleeve. How marvelous it would have looked in cranberry or peach. A mourning country was terrible, almost as bad as a mourning couple.

Mrs. Hessing came forward. "Oh, dear. Hessing's project...protégé and his wife have arrived. Mr. Norton, I tried to get the prince's, I mean our new king's mulatto, Mr. Bridgetower to come and keep you company. But he was too busy, probably playing the violin at court. Do you play, Mr. Norton?"

Barrington opened his mouth, and then closed it for a moment. He looked truly at a lost to respond, so not his usually quip filled self. "I'm not musical, ma'am."

Amora gripped his arm and slipped between them. "We are delighted to be here, Mrs. Hessing.

"Norton, Mrs. Norton," Mr. Hessing plodded forward and took her fingers and kissed it. He held them a little long within his sweaty mitts.

Barrington thawed and retrieved her palm. "Hessing, Mrs. Hessing, I'd like to introduce you to my mother-in-law, Mrs. Tomàs."

Mrs. Hessing smiled. "Oh, so you won't be lonely or give in to mischief. You brought your own brood. Wait until you see the jellies, Mr. Norton. All the colors and flavors of the rainbow. I'm sure you can appreciate that."

"Colors. Great. I can't wait to see them." Barrington nodded to the lady as Amora laced her fingers with his towing him from the hall.

Her heart thawed a little, remembering how hard he worked at the law, and how he graciously suffered small minds.

As if he remembered himself, he released her hand and moved a lonely few feet from her.

No. She'd be of use to him tonight.

She moved to him and laid jittering fingers on his sleeve. "Let's find the dowager."

He smiled at her and covered her palm with his. A charge swept through her. She had to admit to missing him.

These past weeks, he was in the same house, sharing the same roof, but she'd been too afraid to reach for him. If she had, what would keep her strong if she disappointed him again? No, it was better to return to Tomàs Manor. There, she could continue growing her own strength and find her own path.

Yet, at Hyde Park and Whitby, she'd seen a side of him that was accepting and vulnerable. Could he understand weakness or indecision? Would things revert to their normal imbalance, him strong, her weak?

"I forgot to tell you, Amora. You look lovely tonight. Very lovely."

She pulled an ostrich print fan from her silk reticule. "With everyone in shades of black, you must be happy?"

He pulled close to her ear. "I don't need to know the hue, if you smile. That's all I need."

Her cheeks warmed, and she pivoted toward the crowd. "There is the dowager and Mr. Charleton."

A groan slipped his lips. His steps slowed. At a pace a little faster than a drag, he allowed her to lead them to the widow and her son.

As her son frowned and moved away, Barrington

bowed to the old woman.

"Ma'am, this is my mother-in-law, Mrs. Henutsen Tomàs. She accompanied my wife and I tonight."

"I know of the famous Mrs. Tomàs and her girls." The dowager looked over her spectacles toward Barrington and then in her son's direction. "I trust you two will not make sport of this evening. Mrs. Hessing wouldn't be as agreeable."

She rotated in her chair. Her grey silk skirt swished with the effort as the egret plume of her turban waved. She twisted back toward Mama. "Henutsen, where ever did you get that name? That's unusual."

Her mother smiled with her almost polite face. "It's Egyptian. But you know that."

Amora shot her mother a look, pleading with her to be nice, but there was little hope for that. So she intervened making her voice low and sweet. "Dowager Clanville, the name is for a queen from the fourth dynasty. A time of peace and prosperity in Egypt."

"Peace, you say." Barrington's whisper vibrated Amora's ear, as he tapped on her arm. He turned as if to withdraw, but she wouldn't let him. She needed to make sure his relationship with his best client remained intact. That was pivotal to her part of the bargain. She still had something to prove.

"Ma'am, I am so glad that you've allowed me to have my husband back, even for a short time. A sweet pleasure having him about and not missing our outings to draft your documents."

"Well, it's been a slow time, but Mr. Norton, there are some things I'll need your advice upon next week." She squinted above her long quizzing glass. Will you spare him, Mrs. Norton?"

"I will for you, ma'am." Trying to embody a picture of grace and tact, she lifted her chin as she curtsied, then took Barrington's arm.

His strong gaze sent her pulse racing, but the smile on his face disappeared. He released her. "Ah, Vicar Wilson. Let me make room for you."

"Good evening. Mr. Norton, Mrs. Norton, Mrs. Tomàs." The vicar tugged on his patterned waistcoat and puffed up his chest. "My favorite family. Nothing I like more than dancing. Shall we, Mrs. Norton?"

She lifted her gaze to Barrington as if she needed his permission, but he claimed Mama's hand. "Let me find Mrs. Tomàs a place to sit."

"Now, Mr. Norton, I'm not so old. I still enjoy a set." She whipped her puce trimmed fan. "But a good seat out of the traffic would be welcomed."

The vicar lent Amora his arm, but she stopped and watched Barrington's strong figure disappear amid the crowd.

"Mrs. Norton?"

She rubbed her temple and moved toward the vicar but stopped, bumping into Cynthia Miller.

"Ah, Mrs. Norton." The redheaded vixen put a hand on her hip. "It's a shame you've left lonely Mr. Norton alone in favor of a poor vicar with children. I suppose an instant family is better than none."

Only a heartless harlot could be so hate-filled. "Miss Miller, I've no time for your folly."

Cynthia giggled as she adjusted her creamy oriental fan. "Maybe Mr. Norton will have a moment for me now. The dear man looks quite forlorn."

Tired of her threats and her hints of whoring, Amora stepped close to the laughing woman. "Take him if you can. I don't think Barrington plays with trash."

Almost smiling, Amora left Cynthia sputtering with scarlet cheeks and traipsed to the vicar. He looked quite well in his dark coat and pantaloons, but he wasn't Barrington. It hit her hard squarely in her heart how much she'd miss her husband once they separated. If he turned to Cynthia, it would cut like broken glass.

But Amora was abandoning him. It was unfair to expect Barrington to have no one.

"You look very pretty this evening." Vicar Wilson's fingers slipped along her lacy satin gloves as he led her to opposite positions in the quadrille. "But I don't think I'm the partner you want tonight."

She shot him a nod of acknowledgment and kept her gaze from seeking Barrington. "Vicar, you are the only one to have asked."

"Call me, Samuel. You and your mother, have taken to me like a brother." He spun her in the reel and exchanged spots. "As to your current problem, here's a little brotherly advice. A determined woman can do the asking. That Miss Miller seems determined."

Glaring at him wouldn't be proper, so she concentrated on her steps. "It's not done, Vicar Wilson."

He twirled her again, but made a misstep. "I suppose you are right, but is it not better to take some measure of control over your life, your home?"

She stopped and looked up into his earnest face. "What are you trying to say?"

"We men do make mistakes. It would be a shame to condemn someone forever, especially when they seek repentance."

His head craned in the direction Barrington and Mama had traveled. "Forgiveness is a gift everyone needs from time to time."

A sigh left her lips. What did she want of Barrington? Mutual Forgiveness? Another chance at their marriage? Could she risk it?

She stopped dancing, dipped her hand into her reticule, and twisted her notes about her fingertips. Each folded piece of foolscap offered a reminder of the present. One giving the date. Another, that she was free. A few more saying stay aloof, listen not to a weak heart. The notes were all she had without Barrington's daily reassurance.

Beaming down upon her, Samuel cast a breath-stealing smile. "Whatever you decide, know I only want your best."

"Go do your politicking, Mr. Norton. Amora says you're so fond of it. I will be fine here." His mother-in-law took a seat and sipped her raffia punch.

"Oh, not tonight. I need to convince London that the Norton household is united." And too much trouble lurked about. From his post along the wall, he could watch Amora and make sure she was not bothered by Charleton or too delighted by Wilson. Well, on the second count there wasn't much that could be done, but he could hope the man stubbed his toe or something.

"You look sad." Mrs. Tomàs's voice rose over the noise of the crowd. "I wish there was something I could do to help."

"You could've kept the separation paperwork until the morn instead of handing them to me right before we left for the ball." Seeing the parchment made it too true, too final. He and Amora would actually part. He tweaked his spectacles, his mood fouling again. "No, you've done enough. My compliments to your solicitor. I found the passage regarding the provision for minor children particularly piercing."

The woman colored a bit. "Yes, he's quiet knowledgeable, very accurate."

"Too accurate." He ignored the funny lift of her eyes and motioned as if he'd been stabbed in the gut. "The agreement only lacked a section on breaking a neck at a winter fest. Too thorough, madam. Cruelly thorough."

Her smile waned. "You are so like Mr. Tomàs, without understanding sometimes. Don't sign them. Don't separate. It's obvious you still love her."

Barrington rubbed his face. "So five years later, I have your approval."

"I will not lie. I did not think you good enough. Amora has the graces to be a duchess." She grasped his arm. "I wanted someone with purer blood. I didn't want her to face the scrutiny of always being an outsider, always being considered less than."

"Is this suppose to be an endorsement?"

"Hush, you fool. I'm trying to be nice. There will always be someone who will limit you. You can't control that. Let the love I see in you be the guide."

He put a palm on the good pharaoh's fingers. "I wish she could see it."

Mrs. Tomàs smiled, not like an alligator about to eat its prey, but a nice smile. She seemed rejuvenated these past weeks being Amora's confidant. Her onyx hair was coiffed high. Her delicate cheekbones held smooth timeless dark bronze skin. She could be no more than ten years his senior, but looked even younger. Even in this world where the lighter the skin the better, no one could miss Mrs. Tomàs's beauty.

His Amora would age well. If only she'd let him be a part of her life. If she could return his love, he wouldn't need anything else, not even children to be complete. He knew that now.

Barrington stopped gazing at his wife and the vicar and caught sight of Lord Cheshire plodding in his direction.

Oh, Barrington completely forgot the duke's request. His hands had been pretty full. The duke would have to understand.

Before the man could reach him, his duchess claimed his arm. The couple started the next set.

Barrington would send him a note to arrange a meeting. If Smith's last words could be trusted the Dark Walk Abductor might be a peer or a person of influence. Barrington knew he wasn't less than, but he wasn't stupid. He'd need help in navigating a politically charged indictment.

As Barrington adjusted his post, he saw Charleton. Unlike the duke, the man came at him full bore. You'd think mutually blackened eyes would be sufficient.

The golden haired lecher stopped in front of him. "Well, Mr. Norton. What are you doing hiding over here in the corner?"

"I was counting my blessings. I'm sure you've come to aid me."

Charleton scanned back and forth. "You let the vision, your better half, spend time with another man?"

Barrington failed at not gritting his teeth. "My wife has her own mind. She chooses her friends."

Adjusting his dark waistcoat with gold threading, Charleton chuckled. "Now that is the one you need to watch. The vicar has charmed all the women in St.

George. The widower needs to select his next wife and give the rest of us a respite."

Barrington balled his fist. Separation or not, Wilson better not have those ideas when it came to Amora. "Change the subject. I am not in the mood to stop beating you senseless."

The golden baboon laughed anew. The large blackened buttons of his waistcoat jingled. "Norton, you half-breed, you always come unglued over Miss Amora Tomàs."

"Her name's Norton." And would remain so even if she no longer wanted him. Flashy fool. Barrington's temper simmered. "We are both of African descent, why does my blood bother you, but you claim to want her?"

"Simple man. It doesn't bother her. Say a few choice words to you and you forget your accomplishments. It's quite fun to see the great barrister with my mother's ear act like a fool."

Could one beat someone senseless and take their words to heart at the same time? Probably not.

The foppish man belly laughed, then half-pivoted toward the dancing couples. "Well, at least you finally remembered what a diamond of the first water you have. Hopefully putting away tarnished things."

"Stop. Miss Miller has made mistakes. We all do foolish things when we are young."

Charleton squinted at him, rocked back on his heels. "That is true. I tried to steal Amora. We all tried, but she floated away."

Barrington's heart pounded. It had to be beating louder than the music. Was Charleton admitting to abducting Amora? "What are you saying? Did you hurt her?"

"You are insane if you think I touched a hair on her lovely head. Only a crazed person would." Charleton opened his mouth and released another series of laughs. Then his gaze drifted to the left. His face drained, his pale white complexion became even whiter. "What's he doing here?"

Barrington turned.

Lord Clanville, the dowager's oldest son, strolled into the room.

Great. Two Charletons. More annoyance. "What makes the reclusive earl show?"

The lecher whipped his hand through his light hair. "I shouldn't have teased him about almost kissing your wife. Excuse me." He headed in his brother's direction.

Lord Clanville, a tall, athletic man, seemed to peer around the room.

Polite gasps sounded. The dark eye patch poorly masked the burns to his face.

Charleton grabbed the earl by the shoulders and pulled him out of the room. The rake seemed almost frightened by his brother's appearance. Well, let them both be gone.

Air. Barrington couldn't stomach being a wallflower much longer. "Mrs. Tomàs, I need relief from the heat."

"Now you decide to move?" She nodded as her palm tapped on the smooth tabletop.

He swiveled and bumped into Amora. His arms went about her waist to steady her. "Excuse me."

Her mouth opened, a gasp released. "I'm fine."

Her long fingers crept up his lapel and straightened his cravat. "Did you quarrel with Charleton? You look cross."

The stroke of her fingertip on his skin fevered his

brow.

He clasped her palm and tugged it to his heart. "Just counting the seconds to spend the rest of the night with you."

She pulled her hand free and waved her fan. One of the flutters of the pleated fabric almost hit him.

"Amora, this is a public place so you should have no fears of deeper intimacy."

Her eyes stretched wide. "I'm not afraid."

He straightened and looked over her head. "Where's the vicar? I thought he claimed your dances."

"One of the matrons of St. George's came for him. He must do his share of politicking, too."

With as easy of a smile as he could manage, he held his hand to her. "This is probably one of the last times you'll stand up with me. Indulge me. Let's show London we are united. I want to dance with my wife and pretend that the prettiest woman in the world loves me, flaws and all."

The rhythm throbbed as the violins whizzed a Scottish tune. He tapped his slipper to the music and tried to appear at ease. Very difficult with her hint of lilac enticing him to lean near and nibble her neck. "Shall we?"

"Very well." She put away her fan and took his extended elbow.

With the slight touch, something surged his arm through the wool of his tailcoat and broadcloth of his shirt. Never more aware of her curves, the silk of her skin, he spun her in the reel. All of London could burn. Rivals could fend for themselves. Every one of his clients could stay in crisis. Close friends with wayward siblings, all would have to wait. His gaze, his time, was Amora's alone.

The final coupling passed, and they now stood at the end of the line. She smiled at him. Her lips curled up as she caught her breath.

He filled his own lungs. "Shall we risk another?" He held out his hand again.

"If we must." She took it and nothing mattered anymore.

The music turned to another lively tune, something familiar. Her small smile dimmed a little.

He recognized it. "Haydn?"

"It's...It's the prelude to his first suite." Her voice sounded choppy, almost muted.

His hand tightened on hers. "Your father. Didn't he use to play this?"

"Yes." She lifted wide violet eyes. Sadness and something else clouded those perfect gems, yet they were still more lovely than the earrings he'd purchased earlier.

"Let's get some air." He took her in his arms and waltzed her onto a balcony.

She pulled a handkerchief from her reticule and dabbed her face. "It's been so long since I heard that. I shouldn't be so emotional."

He drew his hand along her cheek. "You were taken so soon after your father's death. Maybe you haven't finished mourning."

"I miss him so. He always protected me."

He pivoted and stared out at the thick clouds in the night sky. "I've certainly done a poor job of it."

Tugging on his arm, she made him turn. "Let's not discuss who did a poor job. We both did. This night is to be one of unity."

"Yes, unity." A lantern hooked to the wall cast light

about her. So pretty. He slid his arms about her and slowly pulled her near. "Our first kiss was on a balcony. Maybe that's why I love them so. Could our last be here too?"

Her mouth opened. "I don't know."

"Just one." He bent his head and let his breath cascade her ear. With his cheek, he nudged her turning her face up.

His heartbeat slowed to a crawl as her eyes closed, and her wondrous lips parted.

"Mr. Norton, there you are." Cynthia Miller's voice.

He winced at the lyrical noise and Amora pulled away.

"That is you and Mrs. Norton." She pattered close. "So happy to see you."

Barrington spun and put Amora between them, but kept a protective arm about his wife's middle. He wasn't going to go home smelling of anything but lilacs. "Good evening, Miss Miller. Mrs. Tomàs is here too. You should *go* say hello."

"I am to sing after dinner. Will you and *Mrs. Norton* get a good seat for the performance?"

"Miss Miller, I'd like a private moment with my wife."

Amora put a hand on his forearm. "Of course we will. You run along and save us some."

"I'll do that." A pout filled Cynthia's face. "Mrs. Norton, it's good to see you. I've heard you've been busy spending time with handsome widowers."

"Rumors starting again." Amora's voice fell to a whisper. "Evil rumors."

His gut twisted. Lies had made him side against his wife before. Not this time. Pulling Amora closer, he leaned down and kissed her cheek. "Miss Miller, my wife is very generous, but her honesty and faithfulness should never be questioned. As a favor to me, tamp down any tittle-tattle you might hear. No one should taint her kindness."

A wide frown swallowed Cynthia's countenance. "I'll do that for you." She pivoted and left. The shutting of the doors sounded odd like a slam.

Amora released a heavy sigh and moved from him leaning on the rail. "Go ahead. Ask your questions about the vicar."

"The only question I have is about that kiss of ours."

She shook her head and seemed to stare at the brass sconce fastened to the wall bricks. Her fingers slipped into her reticule, and she tugged out a folded piece of foolscap. Her lips moved as if she chanted something. What was it?

Their moment had faded. Why couldn't he have kissed her before Cynthia made her wary again?

"Can we leave, Barrington? I thought that it would be easier tonight. Since you knew of the abduction, my fear of someone saying something to make you hate me was gone. I'm just not meant to enjoy balls…or anything. At least, I was of use to you tonight."

It felt as if Charleton darkened his daylights again. He was so close to heaven. "The dinner hasn't been served. I need you to be patient, just a little longer, for my mentor."

"You needing me." She chuckled as she smoothed her temples then paced to the balcony doors. "We should go back."

"Without your help, how will I find Sarah? The magistrate told me of two more women with first names of Sarah, each reported missing the summer of your abduction."

Her hand fell away from the knob, and she turned to him. "This is to delay me from returning to Clanville."

"If you leave, I won't be able to determine which one is your friend. I need you."

Her brow crinkled as if she thought long and hard over the matter. "It's probably another liar."

"No, these women are very much like you, taken by a dark force. I won't lie. I would love for you to stay and forget separating next week. I've lived like a hermit in my own home, hoping for a small piece of encouragement, but you haven't changed your mind. I understand, but this is bigger than you or me. It's a chance to bring justice by figuring out who the abductor is." He held out his arm to her.

She batted it down with her fan. "So we'll work together a little longer, then separate?"

"I am giving you power, Amora. Isn't that what you want? To be needed and to feel as if you have control. Help me find the fiend."

"I don't know what to do." She yanked a note from her reticule too quickly. It dropped onto the covered buckle of his shoe.

He reached for it and read, *Remember to Be Aloof, Don't Sway*. He crushed the paper and stashed it in his jacket. Maybe he should pen a few. "You don't have to answer now. There's a week before you are destined to Clanville. Perhaps we can locate one of them."

Large violet eyes lowered. "It's a little cold out here. We should go back."

"Of course." His shoes dragged. Leading her back to Mrs. Tomàs felt like miles. Then he spied the amiable vicar chatting and laughing with his mother-in-law.

His arms numbed as he helped Amora sit. Tramping

over London locating hurt women would be far from romantic. The last time he could hold his wife with passion had just passed.

The vicar stood and came close. "Mr. Norton. There is a Mr. Beakes waiting for you in the foyer. He said the runners have found *a location*. Whatever does that mean?"

Might as well be now. Too much frustration pumped into his veins to stay at Hessing's ball. Barrington rubbed his eyes above his spectacles. *Beake's note.* He'd completely forgotten about it when the magistrate gave him two more *Sarahs*. "Excuse me, I must cut my evening short."

Amora gripped his hand. "One of the women? You found her?" She stood. "I should come with you."

Feeling as if the floor beneath him had opened and swallowed him whole, he closed his eyes for a second, then put her palm into Wilson's. "I want you safe. Vicar, take the ladies home for me."

A smile as wide and as irritating as possible filled Wilson's face. "It will be my pleasure."

He leaned close to his mother-in-law. "Mrs. Tomàs, I'll sign the formal separation tomorrow."

Not looking back, Barrington plodded to the foyer. London should've burned. As he gathered his things from the footman, he watched the dowager's sons arguing in a darkened hall. The musicians' loud play obscured their words, but the hand gestures, Charleton's wild fists, Clanville's thick gloves slapping the air. A very strong disagreement.

Not Barrington's concerns. Protecting Gerald Miller's memory, that's where he needed to put his efforts.

"Mr. Norton." Mr. Beakes ran toward him. "You didn't respond to my note, but I knew you needed to know. We found the man calling himself Miller. He's locked in

Bedlam. We are going for him tonight. I'll await the runners, then seize him. You can meet us at the magistrate when we bring the fiend."

Beakes yanked the revers of his dusty dark greatcoat. "I've better news. I think this man's responsible for an old murder of a milkmaid from your part of England, Clanville. So it's not just fraud he'll be answering for."

He nodded as Beakes, all smiles, plodded with chest puffed out into the night. At least the impostor wouldn't hurt Miss Miller anymore. Gerald had to be smiling down on him for this, taking care of his little sister, protecting her from a possible murderer.

If only Barrington could see the fool's face when the runners seized him.

Maybe he could.

Tugging on his beaver dome, he formulated a plan. If James could get him to Bedlam first, he could see justice in action. The law was his salvation. Focusing on that and not drowning in the hopelessness of his marriage, that had to be a better use of his time. Perhaps, it'd give Barrington a face to darken to extinguish the flames burning within his soul.

Chapter Eleven: Choice and Consequences

Barrington tugged on his gloves and hat as he trudged away from the carriage. James parked at a distance to give Beakes and his men plenty of space. While his solicitor had always been fair-minded, the men he used weren't. Being caught between their thirst for violence and the zealotry wouldn't be prudent. And defending himself or striking out like he'd done with Charleton could prove deadly.

Fog had rolled in shrouding his angry heart. Good. Only lovers needed stars, not fools. Passing through the high stone gate and then trudging across the dirt lane, he began to rethink things. Vengeance was the Lord's, not an angry man's, one frustrated over the impending loss of his wife. He stood on the stone steps of the old Bethlehem Hospital and looked out at the cloudy black night at the grounds of Bethlehem hospital, Bedlam, as everyone called it. Beakes and his associates were nowhere to be found.

Good old James knew every short cut through London. The scent of refuse mixed in the thickening air, adding more misery to Barrington's miserable thoughts. The temptation to spend a few minutes with the villain before they dragged him off to the magistrate and then to foul Newgate prison cut through him again.

Flipping up the collar on his greatcoat and smashing down his hat brim to shadow his face, his fury flamed. With leather gloves concealing his hands, it wouldn't be so easy to separate him from Beakes's runners. No one would be able to note that one of Old Bailey's barristers stole the role of judge and jury. He slouched his shoulders and marched up the final step. The heavy door opened easily. He half expected to see a lunatic show of the patients, but that practice had been abandoned years ago.

Nothing but an austere dimly lit lobby greeted him.

A lad, barely up to his waist, swept the floor.

"Young man, I need to see an inmate." He held up a guinea.

The boy leaned his broom against the wall. "Sir, it's late. Most have settled."

A wail filtered from the dark hall in front of Barrington. The gut wrenching sound cut through his middle. "This won't take but a few minutes. Is your administrator here?" He took out another guinea.

The lad took the coins and stuffed them into his pocket. "No. I'm in charge at night. Do you have a name, sir?"

Barrington scratched his head. He wasn't going to toss his own or Gerald's name and dishonor his dead friend. He pulled out another coin. "I'm not sure, but he's related to Miss Cynthia Miller."

The lad's eyes widened. "The beauteous lady comes after her performances to feed 'm. Such a woman."

Cynthia was a remarkable lass, yet how could she be taken in so wholly? "Show me whom she visited."

Barrington headed toward the long hall, but the boy put a hand on his elbow, then opened a creaking door at the side. "No, sir. That way. Up the stairs."

Not with the rest of the crazed inmates? Barrington followed. His gut swirled with concern for his best friend's sister. Cynthia must be paying a great deal of money for this sham man. Heat roiled inside as his low heels pounded against the treads.

A failing wall candle lit their path as the fellow led him up several twisting treads to the second floor. This area was cleaner and quieter than the bowels of Bedlam.

His guide stopped in front of the third door in the corridor. "You won't have much of a conversation with him."

"Why?"

The boy unlocked a door. "He's barely awake, never speaks. Got to feed him most days. The singer pays me good to make sure of it. Go in."

"This won't take long." Barrington dropped another guinea into his guide's hand before pressing inside. "Go back down, forget I've been here. Things could get dicey as I talk to this man."

"I've got to see about the screamer." The boy left him.

Good. No witnesses. This was personal. The clod impersonated his friend, the man who died saving Barrington. It was better to have no one who could stop him.

He stepped to the door. His fingers pulsated within his leather gloves, every frustration of the past weeks wrapping about each digit. He wanted to punch through the wood, break it into shards like all his mistakes.

How dare someone impersonate Miller.

How dare someone hurt his poor sister.

How dare some fiend abduct Amora.

How dare she not forgive Barrington.

Explaining to the runners why this liar had fresh bruises wouldn't be too complicated. Those ruffians of Beakes wouldn't care.

Barrington pushed open the door. It flung wide and hit the wall with a thud, but no one moved inside.

A shadow hovered in the corner. The villain, the devil incarnate.

Fumbling in his pocket, Barrington found a flinty match and struck it against the wall. The ensuing light highlighted chains.

A hint of sulfur filled his nostrils as the glow between his fingers snuffed. "What's your name?"

The answering silence brought his blood from simmer to full boil. He reared back and opened the door fully. Light flooding from the hall illuminated a man in a long nightshirt, bare feet. His face hung low, still hidden in darkness.

How could someone sit chained in blackness? Was the man mad? How could a crazed person fool Cynthia?

Rocks of confusion collapsed upon his gut, crushing his logic. This must be some very twisted game. He marched closer and kicked the man's foot.

The fellow didn't move, didn't turn his head.

Was he dead?

Barrington stooped and angled the inmate's face to the light.

Vacant almost soulless eyes looked back at him, but air went in and out of the imposter.

Striking another match, he let the sulfur orange light

highlight the liar.

The cleft in the chin.

The nose broken in a youthful indiscretion during a bar fight.

The match burnt Barrington's gloved fingers as it died. Wrenching his hand in the air save the leather, he stood tall and paced.

It couldn't be.

It wasn't possible.

But it was.

The man chained to a Bedlam wall was Gerald Miller. His dead friend lived.

"Nor..." The bag of bones blinked, wriggled a hand in the loose iron bracelet barely clinging to his wrist.

Pulse threatening to collapse, he backed away. He fled the room but stopped at the stairwell. What had he done? The runners would soon arrive for Miller. The man who saved his life was going to be tossed into horrid Newgate. In his crippled condition, it would be a death sentence.

But Beakes said this man was a killer.

Barrington shook his head, clearing his rattled reasoning. No way on God's earth could Gerald Miller kill. He was a lousy shot in the war, barely harmed a fly when they fished, and took a bullet to save Barrington.

His mind spun to the battlefield, the memory of that grisly day Miller died to him.

Barrington wiped sweat from his brow and thought of lovely Amora. She'd do anything to find her Sarah, and the renewed fear for her friend had made Amora sickly. Barrington had just condemned his.

Whatever this conspiracy was, the truth would die with Miller, well, die again with an innocent man he sent to Newgate.

Miller needed to vanish and quickly.

Barrington dashed back into the room. Working fast, he slid the man's boney arms from the iron shackles. With a grunt, he tossed him over his shoulder and carried him like a sack of flour to the stairwell.

With the breath he could muster from his stunned lungs, Barrington blew out the candle. Darkness collapsed upon everything. Feeling his way, he started for freedom.

Round, round, and down, Barrington lugged and hopped and crashed into the wall. Shaking off the sting, he made a final leap to the last stair tread.

Catching his breath, he pressed on the door as lightly as possible so the hinges wouldn't announce them. The crack exposed the foyer and the shadows of five men.

An impatient curse flew. Beake's voice.

The solicitor and four others stood a few paces from the stairwell. If they came this way, they'd catch Barrington.

Beakes's runners were ruthless. They'd fill Barrington with lead shots and probably Miller too. Those men would only see black skin, a thief deserving death, not a gentleman trying to save a friend. All Barrington's work to prove himself as an equal to any would be in ruins. The project Hessing's so aptly called him would be over. No winning legacy of hard work. All would be erased by this folly.

Heart gonging like cymbals, he waited and mouthed a prayer. *Pass another way*.

At a snail's pace they moved. One reached for the knob.

His lungs constricted, flipping out of his chest. He

braced for the end. It was all over. Amora's protection, his career, his honorable name, everything.

Lord, please. I repent. Let them not kill Miller again in the crossfire.

"This way!" Beakes's harsh command stopped the knob from turning and the door from opening to reveal them. "The keeper is probably in his office."

The clop-drop knocks of boot heels faded. They must've gone down the hall.

Air barely forced itself into Barrington's deflated chest. He'd breathe later when Miller was safe. As silently as possible, he eased from the stairwell and flew through the door with his best friend dangling down his back.

They slipped into the blessed night and headed for the high walled gate surrounding Bedlam. On the other side was freedom. The moon glowed but God's foggy cloak shrouded them, hiding them from discovery. Where to go? What to do? The runners could find Miller missing any moment.

Pulse pounding. Head throbbing. Common sense shredding. Barrington's feet started to the gate. Back aching, hip locking, mind gone, he eased Gerald to the ground. "You have to walk to my carriage, man. We have to look normal on the other side of the wall."

The stench of horse manure and foul urine hit Barrington hard. He was a lad again, plucking his father from the bushes behind the Clanville tavern. The man was too drunk to know he'd relieved himself fully dressed, too selfish to care about his poor mother or the Norton name.

But Barrington wasn't a boy. He was a man with more than a name to lose. He tapped Miller's face. "Can you hear me? Stay with me. I'll get you out of this."

The bag of bones nodded.

Tugging off his hat, Barrington put it atop the man's head then bundled him into his bulky coat. It swallowed Miller whole.

As he used to walk his drunken father, Barrington angled and supported his friend so passersby would think Miller was inebriated not an escapee from Bedlam.

"March, man, just like we're in formation."

Step after step, heart knocking at every noise, Barrington shepherded Miller through the gate and tugged him all the way to the carriage. Gasping, he waved to James. "Help."

His manservant bounded down from the driver's box and held open the door.

Barrington shoved and stuffed until Miller fell inside.

Sinking against the shut door, he gulped air. Amora's trust in him to do what was right, his career, his family name – Barrington had just lit a match and burnt it all down.

A hand covered his shoulder. He jumped.

It was his James, not Beakes.

His man's face held no smile. Large eyes hovered close. "Do you know what you are doing, sir?"

"No. Gads, no." Barrington wiped sweat from his brow, then tugged loose his cravat. "I fear I've just ruined myself. Get us away from here. Stay off the populated routes. No one can follow us."

James nodded and helped Barrington into the carriage.

Soon they began to move, the pace unhurried, steady as if nothing were wrong. Though Barrington wanted nothing more than to be miles and miles away, this was best to keep suspicion away.

In the dark with Miller prostrate on the floor, Barrington sat back on the seat, his gaze frozen to the window.

Beakes and his men didn't follow. No one trailed them. They'd been spared discovery, but for how long?

He pushed at his chest and ordered his heart to beat a normal rhythm, but like everything in his life, it didn't obey. "Miller, how? Why?"

No answer. Not even a whimper.

As the road changed from dirt to paved to cobble, Barrington slumped in his seat and counted the blessings he'd almost lost, the one's still at stake like his wife's respect. What would he tell Amora? And what was he to do with a wanted man, one half-dead in his senses?

Sneak Peak: Episode III
* * *

EPISODE III

UNVEILING LOVE

A LONDON REGENCY SUSPENSE TALE

VANESSA RILEY

Episode II of Unveiling Love
Length: 8 Chapters (30,000 words)
Summary: The Truth and Shades of Gray

Barrington Norton has always made the right decisions but desperation, lies, and unexpected truths make things go terribly wrong. Can London's top mulatto barrister save Amora, himself, and their loved ones from ruin?

Amora Norton has come to terms with her abduction and forgiven her Egyptian mother of betrayal, but hasn't the strength to do the same for Barrington or God. Can finding a lost friend and discovering an unexpected blessing be enough to make her whole?

Yet, all their efforts to solve the crime of the century may be for naught. A divided couple is the perfect prey for a criminal wanting sins wiped away.

Pre-order/order the next <u>Episode</u> which releases March 2016. Join my <u>newsletter</u> to stay informed and if you liked this please leave a review.

Here's your sneak peak at the next episode.

Chapter One: Trouble and Truth

The cup of warm tea mother made from the peppermint leaves sat on Amora's bed table. If she sipped it, the potion would make her eyes heavy and her lids droop, but sleep was not what she wanted. Every nerve was on edge. Barrington hadn't come home.

A groan welled inside. Why was she worrying about him? The man was levelheaded, detail oriented, and decisive. That's why he couldn't understand weakness or desperation.

She blew out a breath. He'd been so sweet tonight, so gallant, even a bit hurt at her not giving in to a kiss. Oh how she wanted too. The feel of him, with arms holding her tight, was as addictive as opium.

The draw to him would remain no matter how much she wished it to lessen, she knew that now. If not for the irksome Cynthia, she might have surrendered to the heat in his eyes. A last kiss would no doubt lead to another, then to needing him. Then to crushing disappointment on both sides.

She craned her ear to the window glass. Nothing, not

even a lone horse.

Where was he? Had he found Sarah? Was he in trouble?

She tugged her thick woolen robe tighter about her waist and started pacing again. Every noise made her teeth chatter. Her muscles coiled tighter. Oh, Barrington.

Opening her window, she heard nothing, saw nothing except blackness and swirling fog. Maybe if she went down to the parlor, she could peak from behind the curtains for a better view of the street. She plodded to her door but couldn't grip the crystal knob. What would she say to Barrington when he came inside? What if he were hurt, or never returned at all? What if the monster killed him like he promised to? Barrington hurt, dying in a pit.

She blinked her eyes hard as nausea flooded her stomach. Dropping to her knees, she lowered her face into a wastebasket. The duck dinner and maybe breakfast flowed out. When the heaving stopped, she crawled to her vanity and washed her mouth with rose water. The mirror reflected an ashy complexion and lines beneath her eyes. What was she doing to herself?

The monster had disappeared and Barrington could take care of himself. Her husband was strong and courageous. He didn't need her wearing herself to a thread fretting, or worse, losing control of her reason.

Tip, tap, she clapped her nails along the glass top of the vanity, and listened to the repetition ring out in the stillness. The dreadful rhythm of being alone.

Where was he?

Why couldn't she turn off the caring or the fear?

Would this feeling go away or at least lessen when she returned to Tomàs Manor?

She pushed at her spilling chignon and rinsed her mouth again. How could she turn off this part of her heart before it made her that nervous creature again? It wasn't fair to make Barrington or mother suffer if she became so needy.

A creak and heavy footfalls sounded below, but no carriage noises. The front door hadn't opened. Barrington?

Juggling a heavy Dresden rhinoceros and candlestick, she rushed her threshold, turned the knob and slipped to the stairs. The lower level remained dark. Breathless, she pushed forward. Her bare feet slapped against the treads.

Light edged Barrington's study. He must be home. How did she miss his carriage? She pivoted to return to her chamber but then swiveled back. She had to see his face. That would let her know all was well, then her spirit would ease.

Pulse pounding, she trudged down the hall, humming away her angst. *Amazing Grace. How sweet.* She timed her steps and breathing to the rhythm. Tonight, just walking in the dim light of Mayfair unnerved her, sending a shiver to her limbs.

She pressed on his door and opened it.

Her gaze locked onto Barrington. He paced within, and kept moving as if he hadn't noticed her.

Her heartbeat slowed a little. The man didn't seem injured, but his tailcoat held stains. Heavy breathing fled his nostrils. Something was amiss. She cleared her throat.

One look from his silvery eyes, glazed and bloodshot, confirmed everything. The situation was dire. That suffering heart of hers raced anew. "What is afoot?"

He stopped, yanked off his cravat and plodded toward her. Without a word, he took the Dresden and candle from her fingers and stuck them on a close shelf. Snatching her off her feet, he held her.

Startled, her arms went around him too.

He smelled of dirt and sweat. What had he been doing? "Pray, tell me."

"I…" His heart thudded like gunshots. His muscles quaked and tensed within her grasp. "I've ruined us."

She held him tighter, fingering the tension in his shoulders. "That can't be. Not Barrington Norton."

He pulled away and clutched the bookcase. His mouth opened wide, then he grimaced. "I'm not perfect. Never claimed to be."

Always in control, he never looked like this before. Bewildered, almost scattered.

She came to him, drawn by pure need. Except it was him who lacked, him who was in want of strength. "I didn't mean it as censure."

As she soaked in the tumult swimming in his eyes, it was her who had enough to give. "Trust me, Barr. Trust in me."

Extras

Author's Note

Dear Friend,

I enjoyed writing Unveiled Love because diverse Regency London needs its story told, and I am a sucker for a wonderful husband and wife romance. They need love after the vows, too.

These stories will showcase a world of intrigue and romance, a setting everyone can hopefully find a character to identify with in the battle of love, which renews and gives life.

Stay in touch. Sign up at www.vanessariley.com for my newsletter. You'll be the first to know about upcoming releases, and maybe even win a sneak peek.

Thank so much for giving this book a read.

Vanessa Riley

Many of my readers are new to Regencies, so I always

add notes and a glossary to make items readily available. If you know of a term that should be added to enhance my readers' knowledge, send them to me at: vanessa@christianregency.com. I will acknowledge you in my next book.

Here are my notes:

Mulatto Barristers

I couldn't find definitive proof of one, but that does not mean it was impossible. Connections and success bent rules. Such was the case for William Garrow (1760-1840). He was not born a gentleman and didn't go to the best schools. Yet, his success in the courts rewrote how trials would be performed. He introduced the premise, "presumed innocent until proven guilty," and rose to become Solicitor General for England and Wales.

Free blacks in 1800's English Society

By Regency times, historians, Kirstin Olsen and Gretchen Holbrook Gerzina, estimate that Black London (the black neighborhood of London) had over 10,000 residents. While England led the world in granting rights to the enslaved and ending legal slavery thirty years before the American Civil War, it still had many citizens who were against change. Here is another image from an anti-abolitionist.

The New Union Club being a representation of what took place at a celebrated dinner given by a celebrated society – includes in picture abolitionists, Billy Waters, Zachariah Macauley, William Wilberforce. – published 19 July 1819. Source: Wiki Commons

* * *

Notable People Mentioned in this Episode

George Bridgetower (George Augustus Polgreen Bridgetower) was born in Poland on October 11, 1778. The mulatto described as Afro-European was the son of John Frederick Bridgetower, a West Indie's black man and a white German maid. He became a virtuoso violinist whose talents were recognized by the Prince Regent. The prince took an interest in his education and directed Bridgetower's musical studies. Bridgetower performed in many concerts in London theatres like, Covent Garden, Drury Lane and the Haymarket Theatre. In the spring of 1789, Bridgetower performed at the Abbaye de Panthemont in Paris. Thomas Jefferson attended this event. Bridgewater died February 1860.

Harriet Westbrook was the first wife of Percy Shelley. She was abandoned by Lord Shelley when he fell in love with **Mary Wollstonecraft.** On 10 December 1816, Harriet's body was found. She was pregnant when she was drowned in the the Serpentine in Hyde Park, London.

King George III, the king who lost the American colonies, suffered from bouts of mental illness. His son ruled in his stead as the Prince Regent (George Augustus Frederick). King George III died January 27, 1820. Mourning for a King had three parts: deep mourning (eight weeks), mourning (two weeks), and half-mourning (two weeks). During these times, clothing and accessories had to be correlated to the type of mourning.

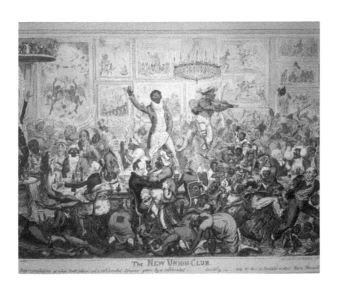

Inter-racial marriages occurred.

The children known as mulattos lived lives on the scale of their education and wealth. Examine this painting. Portrait of a Mulatto by FABRE, François-Xavier. It is from 1809-1810. Portraits were indicative to status and wealth. My screenshot of the image the art once displayed at Arenski Fine Art, LTD London. More information can be found at http://maryrobinettekowal.com/journal/images-of-regency-era-free-people-of-colour/.

This painting of an interracial couple and child, *Pintura de Castas*, from Spaniard and Mulatto, Morisca (1763). Where love exists barriers fade.

Slavery in England

The emancipation of slaves in England preceded America by thirty years and freedom was won by legal court cases not bullets.

Somerset v Stewart (1772) is a famous case, which established the precedence for the rights of slaves in England. The English Court of King's Bench, led by Lord Mansfield, decided that slavery was unsupported by the common law of England and Wales. His ruling:

"The state of slavery is of such a nature that it is incapable of being introduced on any reasons, moral or political, but only by positive law, which preserves its force long after the reasons, occasions, and time itself from whence it was created, is erased from memory. It is so odious, that nothing can be suffered to support it, but positive law. Whatever inconveniences, therefore, may follow from the decision, I cannot say this case is allowed or approved by the law of England; and therefore the black must be discharged."

E. Neville William, The Eighteenth-Century Constitution: 1688-1815, pp: 387-388.

The Slavery Abolition Act 1833 was an act of Parliament, which abolished slavery throughout the British Empire. A fund of $20 Million Pound Sterling was set up to compensate slave owners. Many of the highest society families were compensated for losing their slaves.

This act did exempt the territories in the possession of the East India Company, the Island of Ceylon, and the Island of Saint Helena. In 1843, the exceptions were eliminated.

Glossary

The Regency – The Regency is a period of history from 1811-1825 (sometimes expanded to 1795-1837) in England. It takes its name from the Prince Regent who ruled in his father's stead when the king suffered mental illness. The Regency is known for manners, architecture, and elegance. Jane Austen wrote her famous novel, *Pride and Prejudice* (1813), about characters living during the Regency.

England is a country in Europe. London is the capital city of England.

Image of England from a copper engraved map created by William Darton in 1810.

Port Elizabeth was a town founded in 1820 at the tip of South Africa. The British settlement was an attempt to strengthen England's hold on the Cape Colony and to be a buffer from the Xhosa.

Xhosa - A proud warrior people driven to defend their land and cattle-herding way of life from settlers expanding the boundaries of the Cape Colony.

Image of South Africa from a copper engraved map created by John Dower in 1835.

Abigail – A lady's maid.

Soiree – An evening party.

Bacon-brained – A term meaning foolish or stupid.

Black – A description of a black person or an African.

Black Harriot – A famous prostitute stolen from Africa, then brought to England by a Jamaican planter who died, leaving her without means. She turned to harlotry to earn a living. Many members of the House of Lords became her clients. She is described as tall, genteel, and alluring, with a degree of politeness.

Blackamoor – A dark-skinned person.

Bombazine – Fabric of twilled or corded cloth made of silk and wool or cotton and wool. Usually the material was dyed black and used to create mourning clothes.

Breeched – The custom of a young boy no longer wearing pinafores and now donning breeches. This occurs about age six.

Breeches – Short, close-fitting pants for men, which fastened just below the knees and were worn with stockings.

Caning – A beating typically on the buttocks for naughty behavior.

Compromise – To compromise a reputation is to ruin or cast aspersions on someone's character by catching them with the wrong people, being alone with someone who wasn't a relative at night, or being caught doing something wrong. During the Regency, gentlemen were often forced to marry women they had compromised.

Dray – Wagon.

Footpads – Thieves or muggers in the streets of London.

* * *

Greatcoat – A big outdoor overcoat for men.

Mews – A row of stables in London for keeping horses.

Pelisse - An outdoor coat for women that is worn over a dress.

Quizzing Glass – An optical device, similar to a monocle, typically worn on a chain. The wearer might use the quizzing glass to look down upon people.

Reticule – A cloth purse made like a bag that had a drawstring closure.

Season – One of the largest social periods for high society in London. During this time, a lady attended a variety of balls and soirees to meet potential mates.

Sideboard – A low piece of furniture the height of a writing desk, which housed spirits.

Ton – Pronounced *tone*, the *ton* was a high class in society during the Regency era.

Sneak Peak: Unmasked Heart
* * *

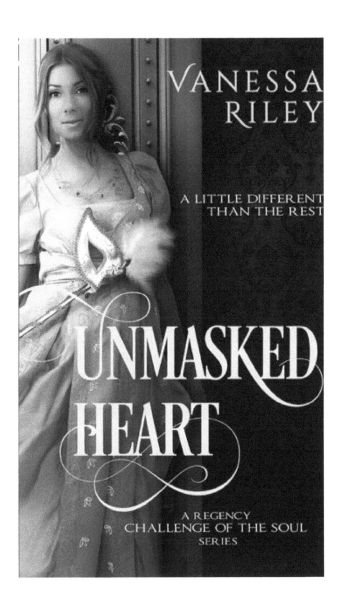

VANESSA
RILEY

A LITTLE DIFFERENT
THAN THE REST

UNMASKED
HEART

A REGENCY
CHALLENGE OF THE SOUL
SERIES

Shy, nearsighted caregiver, Gaia Telfair always wondered why her father treated her a little differently than her siblings, but she never guessed she couldn't claim his love because of a family secret, her illicit birth. With everything she knows to be true evaporating before her spectacles, can the mulatto passing for white survive being exposed and shunned by the powerful duke who has taken an interest in her?

Ex-warrior, William St. Landon, the Duke of Cheshire, will do anything to protect his mute daughter from his late wife's scandals. With a blackmailer at large, hiding in a small village near the cliffs of Devonshire seems the best option, particularly since he can gain help from the talented Miss Telfair, who has the ability to help children learn to speak. If only he could do a better job at shielding his heart from the young lady, whose honest hazel eyes see through his jests as her tender lips challenge his desire to remain a single man.

Unmasked Heart is the first Challenge of the Soul Regency novel.

Excerpt from Unmasked Heart: The Wrong Kiss

Seren adjusted the delicate gauzy silk flowers lining the edges of Gaia's cape. "Wait here until your Elliot arrives. Don't leave this room; I'll come back to find you."

Part of Gaia didn't want to release Seren's hand. Half-seeing things made the room frightening. Her pulse raced. "What if someone else arrives?"

"Tell them the room is occupied. They'll understand." Seren adjusted her silvery sarsenet cape, balanced the scales she hung on a cord in place of a reticule, and smoothed her wide skirts.

Grasping hold of the armrest, Gaia forced her lips to smile. "Good luck to you, Lady Justice. I hope you have fun."

"If you find the love you seek, I'll be happy. You deserve happiness for being you, not someone's daughter. Tell Elliot of your love. Gaia, you need a name and a household of your own, where secrets can't harm you." She gave Gaia a hug. "I want your cup filled with joy."

"Even if my cup isn't pure."

"Your heart is untainted by the past, made pure by salvation. That's what matters." Seren put a hand to Gaia's face. In the candlelight, she and Seren, their skin, looked the same. "Live free tonight."

Seren moved out of focus and left the room, closing the door behind her.

The lime blur of the settee was as comfortable as it was big, but Gaia couldn't sit still. She fidgeted and tapped her slippers on the floor. The ticking of the mantle clock filled the quiet room.

Trying to ignore it, she clutched the ribbons of her papier-mâché mask and straightened its creamy feathers. She stood and, with the pace of a turtle, she moved to the fireplace and strained to see where the limbs of timepiece pointed. Nine-fifteen.

Elliot would be here soon. What would she say to him? Would she remain silent and just dance with him?

She leveled her shoulders. How could she not say her peace, as she looked into his blue eyes? How ironic to unmask her heart at a masquerade ball.

The moon finally broke through the clouds and cast its light into the salon. Whether from the fuzziness of her vision or the beauty of the glow, the window glass sparkled, as did the mirrors and polished candleholders of the small room.

The low tones of the musicians started up again. The jaunty steps of a reel sounded. The tone called to her feet again, and she danced as if she were in someone's arms. The beechnut- colored walls and white moldings swirled as she did.

That set ended and then another and another. She paced in front of the mantle clock. It tolled a low moan as it struck ten. Elliot had missed their appointment. Heaviness weighed upon Gaia, from the crown of her costume's veils to the thick folds of her opal domino.

How ironic to stand in such finery, when Mr. Telfair told her she wasn't worthy. Yet hadn't she schemed with her stepmother and Seren to be here? Gaia should leave. Too many wrongs would never equal righteousness.

Movement outside the room sent her pulse racing. Maybe Elliot had been detained, but was still coming. She wrung her hands and looked to the shining circle on the door, its crystal knob.

The footsteps passed by, the sound diminishing, as did her dreams.

Elliot wouldn't show. He must still think of her as a child, as Julia's hapless sister, as Millicent's plain cousin. Or maybe Julia had told him. They could be laughing about it now.

Sighs and a misguided tear leaked out. She leaned against the burnished mantle. The warmth of the hearth did nothing to thaw her suddenly-cold feet. It was best he didn't show. He'd saved her the embarrassment of his rejection. A mulatto's dance or kiss could never do for him.

The rhythm of a dance set crept beneath the ivory doorframe. Maybe Elliot found a new young lady, whose large dowry like Millicent's made her irresistible to men. Was she in his arms, basking in the glow of his smile, his fun conversation?

The ache in her bosom swelled. Gaia released her breath, stilling her trembling fingers against the sheer veil of her fairy costume. Perhaps she should slip from the room and run into the moonlight of the moors.

The door opened. The strains of violin-play seeped into the salon.

Elliot in his domino cape and ebony half-mask entered the room. "Excuse me," his voice was low, hoarse. He whipped a handkerchief from his pocket and wiped his mouth as he bowed.

Always so formal, but what a pity his melodious voice sounded raspy.

Now or never. She cleared her throat and, in her most sultry manner, she placed her hands to her hips and curtsied. "I've been waiting for you."

"Excuse me, do I know you?" He tugged at the ribbons of his mask.

Waving her arms, she caught his gaze. "Please don't take it off. I won't be able to get through this if you expose your handsome face."

"I see." He stopped, his strong hands lowering beneath the cape of his domino. "Miss Telfair?"

With a quick motion, she whipped up her airy silk skirts and traipsed closer, but maintained an easy distance on the other side of the settee. "Call me Gaia.

We needn't be so formal."

His head moved from side-to-side, as if to scan the room.

"You needn't fret, sir. We are quite alone. That's why I decided to confess my feelings."

"I see."

Must he continue to act as if he didn't know her? The moonbeams streaming through the thick window mullions surrounded him, and reflected in the shiny black silk of his cape. Could he be taller, more intimidating?

Elliot had to think of her as a woman. She straightened her shoulders. "I'm so glad you've come. I know I'm young, but not too young to know my heart."

"Miss Telfair, I think this is some sort of mistake."

Blood pounding in her ears, she swept past the settee and stood within six feet of him. "Please call me Gaia."

"I'll not trespass on your privacy any longer." He spun, as if to flee.

She shortened the distance and caught his shoulder. "Please don't go. It took a lot to garner the courage to meet you here."

With a hesitance she'd never seen from confident Elliot, he gripped her palm and kissed her satin glove. "I know it takes a great amount of courage to make a fool of one's self."

"There's no better fool than one in love." She slipped his hand to her cheek. "Why hide behind mocking? I know you. I've seen your heart. The way you take care of that precious little girl as if she were your own." It touched Gaia, witnessing Elliot helping his brother's household as if it were his own.

"How did you know my fear?" He drew his hand to

his mouth. "You see too much."

Squinting, he still wasn't quite in focus. He shifted his weight and rubbed his neck, as if her compliments made him nervous.

"This is a mistake. We should forget this conversation. A man shouldn't be alone with such a forthright young lady. I will return to the ball." He leveled his broad shoulders and marched to the door, his heels clicking the short distance.

Maybe being so low was freeing. "Why leave?" she let her voice sound clear, no longer cautioned with shyness or regret. "Here can be no worse than out there, with the other ladies readying to weigh your pockets."

His feet didn't move, but he closed the door, slamming it hard. Had she struck a nerve?

He pivoted to face her. "Aren't you just like them, my dear? Weren't all gentle women instructed to follow a man's purse? No? Perhaps torturing is your suit, demanding more and more until nothing remains of his soul."

"Men hunt for dowries, and they know best how to torture someone; ignoring people who want their best; separating friends, even sisters, in their pursuits. The man who raised me did so begrudgingly, just to make me a governess to my brother. Is there no worse torture than to yearn to be loved and no one care?"

"A governess? I think I understand."

This wasn't how she'd expected this conversation to go. Elliot's graveled words possessed an edge as sharp as a sword. He seemed different, both strong and vulnerable. It must be the costumes, freeing them both from the confining roles they lived.

Yet he didn't move. He didn't feel the same.

She fanned her shimmering veil. Half-seeing and disguised, she could be as bold and as direct as Millicent or Seren. Gaia could even face the truth. "I forgive you for not feeling the same."

She'd said it, and didn't crumble when he didn't respond in kind. Maybe this was best. With the release of a pent-up breath, she added, "I wish you well."

He chuckled, the notes sounding odd for Elliot's laugh. "Has a prayer wrought this transformation? Well, He works in mysterious ways."

Maybe it was all the prayers over the years that built up her strength. Amazing. Elliot didn't love her, and no tears came to her. Well, numbness had its benefit. "Good evening. You can go; my friend Seren will be back soon."

When he finally moved, it was to come closer, near enough she trail her pinkie along the edgings of his domino, but that, too, was a cliff she wasn't ready to jump.

"Gaia, what if I'm not ready to leave?"

Her ears warmed, throbbing with the possibilities of his meaning.

"If I am trapped," his voice dropped to a whisper, "it is by your hands."

Her heart clenched at his words. Elliot never seemed more powerful or more dangerous. "I'd hope I, ah, maybe I should be leaving."

He took a half-step, as if to block her path. His outline remained a blur; a tall, powerful blur. "You've had your say, sweet Gaia. Now it is my turn."

This near, she could smell the sweet starch of his thick cravat and a bit of spice. Her heart beat so loudly. Could he hear it?

He drew a thumb down her cheek. "Pretty lady, your

eyes are red. Your cheeks are swollen. What made you cry so hard? And why didn't you find me?"

Something was different about the tone of his hushed voice. There was pain in it. Did he hurt because Gaia had? Could she have discounted the possibility of Elliot returning affections too quickly?

Something dark and formidable drew her to him like never before. "How could I find you? I didn't know you cared, not until this moment."

His arms went about her, and he cradled her against his side. His fingers lighted in her bun. "I'm fascinated with the curl and color of your hair."

Too many thoughts pressed as a familiar tarragon scent tightened its grip about her heart. "Not course or common—"

His lips met her forehead. His hot breath made her shiver and lean more into him. "Never; that's what I've been trying to tell you."

Heady, and a little intoxicated by the feel of his palms on her waist, she released her mask. It fluttered to the floor. Its pole drummed then went silent on the wood floor. She dropped her lids and raised her chin. "I guess this is when you kiss me. Know the lips of someone who esteems you, not your means or connections."

"A lass as beautiful as you needn't ask or wait for a buffoon to find you alone in a library." His arm tightened about her, and he pulled her beneath his cape. The heat of him made her swoon, dipping her head against his broad chest. He tugged a strand of her curls, forcing her chignon to unravel and trail her back. "Now you look the part of a fairy, an all-knowing auburn-haired Gypsy."

He lifted her chin and pressed his mouth against her sealed lips. However, with less than a few seconds of rapture, he relented and released her shoulders.

She wrapped her arms about his neck and wouldn't release him. "I'm horrible. This is my first kiss. I'm sorry." She buried her face against his waistcoat.

His quickened breath warmed her cheek. "Then it should be memorable." His head dipped forward, with the point of his mask, the delicate paper nose, trailing her brows, nudging her face to his. Slowly drawing a finger across her lips, his smooth nail, the feel of his rough warm skin, made them vibrate, relax, then part. "Trust me, Gaia."

She wanted to nod her consent, but didn't dare move from his sensuous touch.

"Let a real kiss come from a man who covets your friendship, who thinks you are beautiful." He dropped his domino to the floor.

Read more of <u>Unmasked Heart</u> at VanessaRiley.com.

Sneak Peak: The Bargain III
* * *

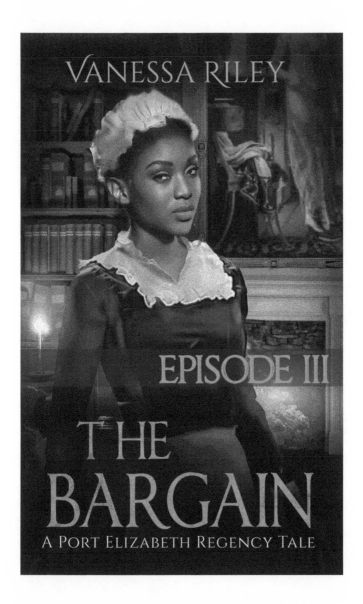

VANESSA RILEY

EPISODE III

THE

BARGAIN

A PORT ELIZABETH REGENCY TALE

Episode III of The Bargain
Length: 11 Chapters (30,000 words)
Summary: Secrets Revealed

Excerpt: The Aftermath of a Kiss and the Xhosa

"Captain," Ralston cleared his throat. "She fixed me up and a number of others."

The baron's lips pursed as he nodded. "Miss Jewell is full of surprises."

His hair was wild and loose. He smelled of beach sand and perspiration. Still frowning, he raised Ralston's arm a few inches from the boat's deck. "Looks like you will live."

"Don't know how much good that'll do me here, Captain. We left here with peace. Why? What happened? And Mr. Narvel?"

"I don't know, but I'm going to find the answers." Using Mr. Ralston's good arm, the captain pulled him to stand. "Get yourself below and sleep. I've got men on watch. Our guns are ready this time for any other surprises."

The sailor shrugged as he tested his shoulder, pushing at the wrapped muscles. "Yes, Sir."

Lord Welling leaned down and took Precious's hand. "You've helped enough, Miss Jewell. I want you to go down below."

She shook her head. "There's more I can do up here."

The baron snatched her up by the elbow. "I insist."

Precious shook free and grabbed up the doctoring supplies. "We're probably going to need these again."

Ralston closed his eyes and grunted almost in unison

with Lord Welling before trudging past the other men laying out on the deck, the one's whose injured legs prevented them from going below. With no rain, they'd be alright under the night sky.

Precious looked up into the night sky that looked like black velvet with twinkling diamonds. Such innocence shrouds this place. So opposite the truth.

"Come along, Miss Jewel. Now." The baron's voice sounded of distant thunder, quiet and potent. His patience, his anger, at so many lost this night must be stirring. He again put his hands around her shoulders and swept her forward.

She didn't like to be turned so abruptly, but stopping in her tracks didn't seem right either. So she slowed her steps, dragging her slippers against the planks of the Margeaux. "What are you doing?"

He stopped and swung her around so that she faced him. "I need your help telling Mrs. Narvel. It's not going to be easy telling a pregnant woman that—"

"Her husband has died at the Xhosa's hands." Precious's heart drummed loudly, like a death gait. Staying busy helping the injured delayed the building grief she had for her friend. Oh, how was Clara to take it?

Lord Welling's lips thinned and pressed into a line. "It's never easy telling a woman a difficult truth or waiting for her to admit it."

She caught his gaze. It felt as if the fire within it scorched her. Suddenly, the smell of him, the closeness of his stance made her pulse race. He wasn't talking about Clara, but Precious wasn't ready to admit anything.

And what would he think if she told him that at that

moment with Xhosa bearing down upon them that nothing seemed more right than to dive headlong to save him. No, Lord Welling didn't need that bug in his ear.

But soon, he'd press. He wasn't the kind of man who waited for anything.

He gripped her hand and led her into the darkness where those stars twinkled in his eyes. "Precious, I need to ask you something."

Chin lifting, she pushed past him and headed for the hole and the ladder below. "We need to get to Mrs. Narvel."

She took her time climbing down, making sure of her footing on each rung, then she waited at the bottom for her employer, the man who in the middle of chaos kissed her more soundly than any one ever had.

His boots made a gentle thud as he jumped the last rungs. When he pivoted, he crowded her in the dark corner, towering over her. "You're reckless, Precious."

She backed up until she pressed against the compartment's planked wall. "I'm not the only one. Taking Jonas to a land of killing, that's reckless."

He clutched the wall above each of her shoulders, but he might as well had gripped them with his big hands. There was no escape from the truth he was waiting on.

Leaning within an inch of her, his voice reached a loud scolding tone. "You're reckless. Wanton for danger."

Her face grew warm and she bit down on her traitorous lips, ones that wanted a taste of him again.

His breathing seemed noisier. His hands moved to within inches of her arms, but they didn't sneak about her. No, those fingers stayed flat against the wood, tempting, teasing of comfort. "You could've been killed. Will you ever listen?"

The harshness of his tone riled up her spirit. "Won't do me no good to listen if you're dead. The least you can say is thank you."

He straightened and towed one hand to his neck. Out of habit, she squinted as if he'd strike her, but she knew in her bones that wasn't to happen. The fear of him hurting her was long gone. Only the fright of him acting again on that kiss between them remained. "What am I to do with you?"

Get the next Episode. Look for all the episodes. Join my newsletter to stay informed.

Join My Newsletter, Free Goodies

Thank you for taking the time to read Unveiling Love. If you enjoyed it, please consider telling your friends or posting a short review (Amazon or Goodreads). Word of mouth is an author's best friend and much appreciated. Thank you.

Also, sign up for my newsletter and get the latest news on this series or even a free book. I appreciate your support.

VR

Let me point you to some free books, just for reading this far:

Free Book: The Bargain - Episode I:

Coming to London has given Precious Jewell a taste of freedom, and she will do anything, bear anything, to keep it. Defying her master is at the top of her mind, and she won't let his unnerving charm sway her. Yet, will her restored courage lead her to forsake a debt owed to the grave and a child who is as dear to her as her own flesh?

Gareth Conroy, the third Baron Welling, can neither abandon his upcoming duty to lead the fledgling colony of Port Elizabeth, South Africa nor find the strength to be a good father to his heir. Every look at the boy reminds him of the loss of his wife. Guilt over her death plagues his sleep, particularly when he returns to London. Perhaps the spirit and fine eyes of her lady's maid, Precious Jewell, might offer the beleaguered baron a new reason to dream.

Free Book: A Taste of Traditional Regency Romances: Extended excerpts of Regency novels (Bluestocking League Book 1)

From some of the most beloved authors of Regency romance come stories to delight. These excerpts, set in the time of Jane Austen, will give you a sip of sweet romance and will leave you eager for more.

Gail Eastwood, The Captain's Dilemma: Escaped French war prisoner Alexandre Valmont has risked life and honor in a desperate bid to return home and clear his name. Merissa Pritchard risks charges of treason and her family's safety to help the wounded fugitive. But will they risk their hearts in a most dangerous game of love?

From Camille Elliot, The Spinster's Christmas:

Spinster Miranda Belmoore and naval Captain Gerard Foremont, old childhood friends, meet again for a large Christmas party at Wintrell Hall. Miranda is making plans to escape a life of drudgery as a poor relation in her cousin's household, while Gerard battles bitterness that his career was cut short by the injury to his knee. However, an enemy has infiltrated the family party, bent on revenge and determined that Twelfth Night will end in someone's death …

April Kihlstrom, The Wicked Groom: When the Duke of Berenford is engaged to marry a woman he's never met, what's a poor man to do? How was he to know she wouldn't appreciate his brilliant scheme?

From Vanessa Riley, Unmasked Heart: Shy, nearsighted caregiver, Gaia Telfair never guessed she couldn't claim her father's love because of a family secret, her illicit birth. Can the mulatto passing for white survive being exposed and shunned by the powerful duke who has taken an interest in her? William St. Landon, the Duke of Cheshire, will do anything to protect his mute daughter from his late wife's scandals. He gains the help of Miss Telfair, who has the ability to help children learn to speak, but with a blackmailer at large, if only he could do a better job at shielding his heart.

Regina Scott, Secrets and Sensibilities: When art teacher Hannah Alexander accompanies her students on a country house visit, she never dreams of entering into a dalliance with the handsome new owner David Tenant. But one moment in his company and she's in danger of losing her heart, and soon her very life.

Join the Bluestocking League in celebrating the wonder of traditional <u>Regency romance</u>.